PAYNE BEFORE

PLEASURE

A Metro City Novel

KATRINA AVANT

Katrina'sWorks
PUBLISHING LLC

Katrina'sWorks
Publishing, LLC

ISBN-13: 9780998218908
ISBN- 10: 0998218901

Payne before Pleasure
Copyright © October 2016
Katrina Avant
Katrinaavant-author.com

Editor
L.R. Clark

Cover Design
Soul Sister Ink

Katrinasworks.com

Chapter 1

Pulling off his latex gloves, Dr. Jon Payne reached for his hospital issued tablet to update his patient's file. The young man, who was still screaming obscenities, was writhing in pain from the one of the night's many gunshots. An irritated nurse glanced in the doctor's direction before administering a shot of morphine into the newly hung IV bag. They both hoped it would take effect immediately to give him some relief *and* shut his mouth.

Looking at the x-rays again; it didn't appear as if the bullet hit anything major. The hot lead had traveled clean through the muscle of his upper thigh, so he would heal nicely. Jon just wished the embattled streets could heal as easily.

The teen was the fourth casualty of the night; a result of a territorial war that had been raging since the imprisonment of the city's former mayor and police chief, Craven Wallace and Warren Allen. Both men were sentenced to multiple life terms for their roles in escalating the crime and corruption that plagued Metro City. Now that the two crime bosses no longer controlled the streets, the city's underbelly was up for grabs and every wannabe gangster was fighting for any and all claimed and unclaimed territory. But if the new district attorney had her way, the dynamics of the streets were about to change.

The nurse glanced at Jon again, but this time with a small smile. The morphine was doing its job. The young man's endless tirade had stopped abruptly as the drug took effect. They both were grateful.

"Do you think the new prosecutor will get this madness under control?" Shelby asked, as they made their way out to the nurse's station. Shelby Kirkland was Metro Regional Hospital's head nurse.

Jon winked at one of the passing female interns before turning his attention to Shelby. "I sure hope so. We can't continue like this night after night. At the rate these bangers are going, they will wipe out an entire portion of the city before it all ends."

Jon shook his head. He hoped the new prosecutor knew what she was doing. The city deserved a period of calm after what the former administration had put it through. He glanced with hope at the flyer tacked to the bulletin board behind the nurse's station. The coffee stained piece of paper contained a photo of the new prosecutor with her back straight and her arms folded. The trendy tailored suit and stiletto pumps belied the sternness of her expression that mimicked the paper's message of taking no prisoners, in her effort to clean up Metro City's mean streets. Considering the D.A.'s photo again, Jon wanted to believe Jess Ashford could heal Metro City's ills for all of their sakes.

Shelby followed Jon's gaze with a resigned sigh. Not because she was contemplating his answer, but because she knew he didn't have a clue as to how she felt about him. But one day, he would look at her as he did the other women in the hospital; as he did the lady D.A. She gave him a last fleeting gaze, before heading up the corridor to attend to her next patient. Jon never saw the longing in the nurse's eyes. He was still eying the prosecutor's photo.

Jess Ashford swept into town with a mission. Her first few weeks on the job hit the criminal element without warning; flooding the income challenged neighborhoods with flyers and billboards announcing the impending end to their violent battles. Jess took over the position slated for former assistant district attorney Garrett Pleasant, who resigned his post to become a full time writer. As the lead assistant prosecutor, he was next in line to become the top district attorney, after his former boss resigned due to poor health. However, Garrett made the choice to leave the world of crime fighting behind when his hit novel, *Criminal Intrigue,* captured the number one spot on the New York Times bestseller's list. Because of his success in taking down the city's former crime bosses, most hated to see him leave, but were willing to give Jess Ashford a chance.

Finally dismissing the flyer, Jon rolled his neck with a grunt. He was tired. It had been a long night and from the looks of things it was about to become longer. Before he could finish stretching, another patient was being wheeled in by paramedics; another gunshot victim. With a quick assessment, he realized his task wouldn't be so simple this time. This one had a gaping chest wound and would require immediate surgery.

Jon pursed his lips. The young boy couldn't have been more than thirteen. What was the world coming to when children regularly entered his ER with gunshot wounds? With no time to consider the child's role in the escalating street war, he barked orders to his team, before racing ahead to prepare for his task. With any luck, he would save the boy's life; but from his preliminary examination it wouldn't be a walk in the park.

◄◊►

It was seven forty-five in the morning and Jon was dead on his feet. He managed to save the young boy's life and he was relieved but weary. If things continued in this trend, he would be back tomorrow night repeating the same scenario, but at least he had the day off for a little R&R.

Yawning, he stopped at the coffee machine before heading to his car; sipping the hot mediocre brew, he drudgingly made his way to the employee's parking lot. The coffee would enable him to drive the short distance to his home where he could grab what he really needed most; a hot shower and a day's worth of sleep. And if fate smiled on him, those precious hours of slumber would be uninterrupted. He'd been working none stop for forty-eight hours and he was exhausted. These were the times he was grateful he didn't have a wife and children to hinder him. He needed quiet. Unlike some of his colleagues, who had family matters they had to attend to, whenever they did manage to drag themselves in from a long shift, he was free to crawl into his bed uninhibited. He didn't envy them.

Jon Payne was a lifelong confirmed bachelor. He enjoyed the company of women—all women—with no desire to change his position. Every woman he dated, tried desperately to readjust his single status, but failed miserably. In the past, he would have randomly selected any willing nurse or fellow physician to satisfy his carnal needs. But after a few hurt feelings among his co-workers, he chose to satisfy those needs beyond the hospital's gossip-mongering walls. Nowadays he trolled for his bed mates at bars and other gatherings; any place that had nothing to do with the medical industry. It may have been easier to choose from the ready pool of partners among the hospital's staff, but after Dr. Lara Guyton, he learned his lesson and learned it well.

In the beginning, everything about Lara was ideal. She was an intelligent woman who understood the boundaries of their arrangement and he fully expected her to adhere to them. They saw each other casually and partook of each other's bodies when the need arose, which was often. But after a few weeks, Lara became obsessive and clingy. At first he thought the behavior would pass and she would get it together and get back on track. So, when it became clear the circumstances weren't going to change, Jon distanced himself from her—thinking the break would end things neatly. Yet instead of ending, Lara Guyton's desperate grasp ratcheted up the drama ten-fold. She became so out of control; she lunged at him with a scalpel while they were in the midst of repairing a spinal injury. No one knew how unhinged she had become until that episode. Due to her psychotic behavior she now resided in a low security mental health compound just outside the city limits.

After the incident with Dr. Guyton, Metro Regional's female staff should have taken her breakdown as an omen to stay away from Jon Payne. But his colleagues wanted him just that much more. Any man who could send a woman as highly educated and regarded as Lara Guyton over the edge, had to be exceptionally good in bed. This way of thinking prompted all those, who had not sampled Dr. Payne's wares, to line up for a chance to follow in her footsteps to find out for sure.

Drowsy, Jon woke up to a ringing phone. He blinked in the darkened room, before his eyes adjusted enough to note the time on the bedside digital clock; confirming he had been asleep for nearly a full eleven hours. That should have been sufficient, but his body was protesting otherwise. Patting the bedside table for his phone, he sat up to see who was calling, before silencing the annoying thing. He just hoped it wasn't the hospital; anyone else could wait until after a few more hours of sleep.

He narrowed his gaze at the caller display; it was his brother. Plopping back onto his pillow, Jon knew what he wanted, so he could definitely wait. Putting the phone on vibrate, he returned it to the table and fell back to sleep.

Chapter 2

Landon Payne frowned when his call rolled over to voicemail. Jon was avoiding him—again. He just wanted some information. And if he gave him what he wanted he would stop bugging him. Landon wanted insight on the new district prosecutor. For some reason, he couldn't seem to get the attractive woman out of his head.

He saw Jess Ashford for the first time in Metro Regional's ER. He was taking the statement of a mugging victim when she appeared to interview the middle aged woman. Landon was taken by her professionalism and a confidence he'd never experienced in any other woman. Her dedication was impressive, since most prosecutors never ventured beyond their offices, let alone come down to an emergency room in the middle of the night to interview a victim. Jess was hands on and he liked that. And it didn't hurt that the woman was voluptuous and beautiful; just his type.

While he was taking in the lady D.A.'s curves, his brother Jon joined them to check on the patient. He watched his interaction with Jess, looking for any hint of familiarity. Either Jon wasn't interested or Jess had shot him down, because the two were polite, but not what he would call friendly. He assumed the latter, because Jon never met a beautiful woman he didn't like and wanted to bed. Furthermore, Jess hadn't been in town long enough for him to use her and drop her, as he was known to do. His self-centered brother was infamously known for leaving a path of broken hearts and hard feelings trailing behind him.

Landon inwardly chuckled at the woman's coolness towards him. At the same time, he was grateful. Since Jon hadn't had his hands on her, he saw this as a sign that he might have a chance. With his brother's womanizing reputation, any woman who turned him down was placed high on Landon's list for consideration. All women weren't impressed by good looks or a man with an MD behind his name, and more than once he tried to explain this to Jon. Contrary to his brother's thinking, some women wanted an actual relationship, instead of boasting creds for sleeping with a doctor. These were the females who looked beyond the shallowness and avoided the bag'em and bed'em types. And he had a feeling D.A. Ashford was one of those women.

It had been over a month since he first laid eyes on Jess, but that minor detail hadn't halted his curiosity. The less he saw of her the more he wanted to. It had taken him weeks to gain enough courage to inquire of the prosecutor from some of his coworkers, who teased him mercilessly over his interest in her. They all assured him the new D.A. was out of his league. After finding no help on the job front, he turned to his brother in hopes of a little guidance in approaching the woman without Jon's usual lecherous anecdotes as an added bonus. He and Jon may have had their differences, but they were still brothers.

Jon, the older of the two, hadn't liked it one bit when Landon decided to ditch law school in favor of the police academy. He felt Landon was far too intelligent to throw his life away to become a lowly paid civil servant. This was another reason why he didn't readily answer his calls. Landon had been on the job for over three years, but Jon was still giving him grief over his career choice.

Landon shook his head. He wondered if his brother would ever get over his decision. As much as Jon wanted him to become a lawyer was how strongly he didn't want to be one. Sure he was smart and could have easily breezed through the necessary channels to become what his family wanted, but that wasn't for him. Being a police officer was his calling whether Jon or any of his other family members understood that.

Without leaving a message, Landon ended the call and shoved the phone back into his back pocket to open the door to one of his favorite eateries, *Randy's Place*. He decided to hit up the city's popular diner for dinner and had hoped Jon would join him, but it looked like he would be dining alone tonight.

Landon maneuvered himself through the crowded restaurant; nodding at a firefighter acquaintance and his girl, before heading for the tables in the back, in hopes of finding his favorite booth available. He grinned when he found that it was. While he settled himself, one of the regular waitresses sought him out. Trudy had been a presence at *Randy's Place* for as long as he could remember and was always a welcomed sight when he ventured inside.

"Hey Landon, how you doing this evening?" Trudy asked while pouring him a glass of water. Trudy Franklin was a brown skinned, older, heavy-set woman who put him in the mind of a loving grandmother. She was a fixture there and everyone loved her.

Landon smiled up at the older woman. "Hey Miss Trudy, I'm good."

"Listen hon, I hate to ask, but as you can see this place is standing room only and you got the last table available. Anyway, I was wondering, if you're not expecting company, would you mind sharing your space with a young woman. This is her first time here and I want to make sure it won't be her last, considering some of the customer's tonight are quite rude." Trudy turned to give the couple three tables over the evil eye. They had been barking demands at her since the moment they arrived.

Landon peered around her to see who she was glaring at and understood immediately. He didn't recognize the woman, but the man he was familiar with. The rude diner was one of the area's reputed gang heads. Both, dressed in over the top hip-hop attire, were sprawled across the space as if they owned the place. The man even had the nerve to have one leg propped up along the edge of the table. He considered asking him to remove it, but decided to wait instead. This might not be the desired table etiquette, but as long as they weren't causing any real trouble, he would leave them be for now.

Returning his gaze back to the waitress Landon shrugged. "Sure Trudy, no problem."

Trudy grinned. "I'll be right back." She hurried off to get Landon's dinner companion, but not before knocking the surprised man's foot off the table as she swept by.

Landon chuckled at the gesture. Trudy didn't need his help after all. While he waited, he eyed the couple once more before dismissing them to scan the menu, even though he knew every entrée listed there by heart. He was still looking over his choices when someone slid into the booth opposite him. Landon glanced up.

The woman seemed nice enough, but with a closer inspection, he thought he knew her. Then it clicked. She was the woman who had been shot inside Ellis Publications some months back. While his sergeant and the other officers were dealing with the crazed woman with the gun, he had knelt to help her female victim. He tried to recall her name. It was Irene or Steen or something like that. He remembered her, because even though she was lying in a pool of blood, she was cursing the shooter the entire time. The lady was tough.

Queen Ella Willis gave Landon a small smile as she settled herself into the booth. She thought it was nice of him to share his table with her. She had just completed her three-month milestone on her new job and decided to celebrate by trying the diner everyone was raving about. But once she stepped inside and saw the crowd, she was about to turn to leave when Trudy stopped her. She promised she would find her a seat and she had.

Queen parted her lips to introduce herself, but blinked at Landon's open stare. She was beginning to think this wasn't such a good idea after all, when Trudy appeared at her side.

"Hon, this here is Landon, one of my regulars; so I know you'll be in good hands," Trudy informed her with a pat on the shoulder. Turning to Landon, "Landon, are you having your usual or are you trying something different tonight?" She gave him a good hearted wink.

Trudy was amused at how the two sat staring at each other. She hoped something good would come out of her impromptu matchmaking. She immediately thought of Landon when she spotted the young woman. She glanced at Landon's dinner companion's left hand and nodded when she confirmed there wasn't a ring there.

"Umm...could you give us a few minutes? I'm sure Miss..." Landon eyed Queen for her name.

"Queen," she provided for her dinner mate.

"Miss Queen would like a moment to look over the menu."

Queen nodded her agreement. "Just Queen, thank you." She smiled up at Trudy.

"Sure, I'll let you two young people have a few minutes." With that Trudy left to take another order.

While Queen turned her attention to her menu, Landon spoke again, "You don't remember me do you?" He could tell how she eyed him that she didn't.

Why would she? She was lying on the floor bleeding out when I came to her aid. I'm pretty sure she wouldn't have cared who was there with her that night.

Queen, tilting her head to one side, gave Landon's face a thorough examination, but couldn't place him. *Should I know him? And if so, from where?*

Feeling more discomfort creeping in, she slowly shook her head in the negative. She was hoping against hope; he wasn't a throwback from her not so distant wild days. There were a few times, after getting a little tipsy, she had taken a guy home from a bar. But if that were the case, wouldn't she remember a man this good looking? She frowned. In the bad old days, she would have been all over him whether she remembered him or not. This latter thought was not comforting at all.

But that was the past. She was trying to better herself after the whole crazy Allison mess and was accomplishing the task quite nicely. Before, she would have all but jumped in the man's lap, instead of being the prim and proper lady of today. She had even traded in her hoochie mama attire for a more conservative look. She had her friend Cymone Tully to thank for that. Cymone never cared for her trampy persona and with good reason. She was just sorry it took a bullet to the gut for her to see the light.

"I was the officer who held your hand while we waited for the ambulance that night you were shot." Landon finally saw recognition in Queen's eyes.

Wide-eyed, she cupped her hands over her open mouth. "That was you? Oh my goodness!" She had totally forgotten about the policeman who tried to soothe her during that terrible time. There she was on the verge of panicking, after realizing her so-called friend had shot her, all because of Allison's disillusion over a man.

"Oh my goodness, thank you!" She couldn't believe it. What were the odds?

Landon shook his head. "You don't have to thank me. I was just doing my job."

Queen held up a hand to stop him from minimizing his role that night. "Nah, uh," she told him shaking her head, "You have no idea how you helped me that night.

After I got through screaming at that nutcase Allison, I realized I was hurt and would have freaked out if you hadn't been there to talk me through it."

She reached out and captured one of his hands in both of hers; giving it a firm shake. "Thank you for keeping me calm." And she meant it. When she came to the realization that Allison had indeed shot her, she thought she was going to die, especially after seeing all the blood that was leaving her body. And the pain, she couldn't have made it through any of it without him.

Letting his gaze slide over Queen's voluptuous body, Landon smiled. If he wasn't so focused on getting with the lady D.A. he would take the time to get to know her better. But he would definitely get her information to file away for future references.

Trudy paused in taking a customer's order, to glance over at the couple. She grinned at the smiles displayed on their faces. They were getting along just fine. And given the chance, she would help them along beyond a mere acquaintance.

Chapter 3

Jessie Rochelle Ashford touched up her lipstick while her companion tucked himself back into his tailored trousers. She wished she could have had more than the quick encounter, but they both were due in court shortly.

She had chosen her newly christened conquest carefully. She made it a point to do an extensive background search on all of her men. She didn't need any surprises, but more importantly, she couldn't afford for anyone to reveal her secret. She always selected men who had just as much to lose as she did, therefore guaranteeing they would keep their mouths shut and the man zipping up his fly was no exception.

During her investigation, Jess discovered she wasn't the only one with secrets. She knew the right questions to ask from the right people; people who were a part of her sordid world. In her discreet inquiry, she discovered James Harrison was a sadist. He enjoyed the terror and pain he inflicted on others in *and* out of the courtroom. Instead of this knowledge scaring her off, it intrigued her. She didn't mind a little pain with her pleasure. She just hoped he could handle her turning the tables on him.

She also discovered the woman in his last relationship had pulled up stakes and skipped town to get away from him. And she by no means thought it was a coincidence that the two landed in Metro City. She heard through the grapevine that James had been quietly inquiring of his lost love's whereabouts, who just happened to be the doctor who tried to kill one of Metro City's prominent surgeons. After further digging, she discovered the two had lived together prior to relocating. Undoubtedly, Dr. Guyton couldn't handle her former lover's brand of play.

Being new to the city herself, Jess had jumped at the chance to take on the vacant position left by Garrett Pleasant. And when it was made known that she would become the top prosecutor until the next election, well that was icing on the cake. It had become past time for her to move on from her last position. If she had stayed any longer, her secret life may have been compromised. Even though she had taken great pains to keep her cover, she knew there was always a chance of discovery. The constant threat of exposure gave her a dual edge: one, it kept her on her toes and two it pushed her to greater heights in her career.

The position in the Metro City's D.A.'s office was a giant step up from her last post as a glorified gopher in another city's prosecuting office. Not liking the underling position, Jess fought and clawed her way into recognition among her peers, as well as the city. Although she worked hard to make a name for herself there, the lead prosecutor didn't take kindly to those who out shined him. And it didn't help that she was a woman dominating in a man's world. After rubbing her boss the wrong way a few too many times, Jess thought it was best for her to move on, before he decided to take an interest in her personal life. Even though it shouldn't matter what she did on her own time, she knew it did matter when it came to a woman's sex life. And she had no doubt that her former boss would have used her proclivities for men against her.

Jess had an unquenchable hunger for the male anatomy, which included the occasional high priced male prostitute whenever she was outside the countries boundaries. Whenever she wasn't working on a case, she was laid spread eagle or bent over a piece of furniture, feeding that hunger. Jess was young, beautiful and talented and she knew it. She wielded these attributes with a level of power that most women couldn't accomplish. With this power came the ruthlessness usually only attributed to men, which made her good at her job among other things.

Jess's newest conquest was a fellow attorney who worked in private practice. They were to be opponents in an upcoming hearing, which if they didn't get a move on they would be late.

Jess's 'lunch' winked at her before quietly leaving her office. She would give him a few minutes before she too would leave to join him in the courtroom. But before she left, she needed to set up an appointment for a 'dinner' date. Sure they would have food, but she would most definitely have the man for dessert.

Chapter 4

The nurses watched Dr. Payne side-eyed as he swaggered up to the nurse's station. Each of them dying to get a taste since the moment they laid eyes on him. Jon Payne was the most sought after single male doctor at Metro Regional. With his tall stature, chocolate brown good looks and available status, there wasn't a woman alive who didn't wonder about the good doctor. And if he thought he was popular before, his stock skyrocketed after Lara went off the rails. His female worshippers speculated that he had to be one hell of a lover to make a woman like her lose her mind. And each and every one of them wanted a sample of what Dr. Lara had the good fortune to feast on; crazy or not. Among the women eyeing Jon Payne was head nurse Shelby Kirkland. Though she did her best not to let on, she too longed for her own session with him.

Once she was hired as head of the nursing staff at Metro Regional, Shelby coolly kept a distant watch on Dr. Payne. Unlike the other nurses, she never allowed her interests in him show. She was much too reserved for that. While the other women were cat calling and drooling over the man, she played it safe by pretending to be uninterested in the popular surgeon. She thought the others were too desperate and immature to deserve a man such as Jon Payne and never participated in the hospital's mass fawning or gossip concerning him. She thought it was absurd the way women all but threw their panties at him; referring to him as 'Dr. Payne before Pleasure'. When *she* snagged Jon Payne, it would be through genuine emotions and not low brow antics.

Dismissing the host of brooding women with a flip of her long brown hair, Shelby rolled her eyes before beginning her rounds.

Jon tried not to allow himself to be drawn into the attention the nurses gave him; especially those he'd slept with. He would occasionally flirt with them, but that was about as far as he was willing to take it. While keeping the women at bay, he couldn't help but notice the dismissive gesture Shelby Kirkland gave him and his audience.

Although she grabbed his attention from the day she started, he was determined to stick to his vow of not dating anyone in the hospital ever again. He had long dismissed the growing number of female admirers; all jockeying to gain favor in his bed as well as his heart. More than once he had woken in the on-call room to find a random female minus her clothing lying beside him while offering up her goods. Before Lara Guyton, he would have gladly rolled over and tasted, but not anymore. With the attempt on his life, Lara had put an end to all that.

Although he missed some of those raunchy days, she had done him a favor in that regard. It had been a mistake to play where he worked. But still, he wondered about the head nurse. She seemed completely unfazed by his charms and it puzzled him.

Since he started his practice at Metro Regional, there hadn't been a woman married or single who hadn't flirted with him at some point and time, but not Shelby Kirkland. She was the exception. He arrogantly wondered if she just wasn't into men. In his mind, it would explain her indifference to him. Or was there something deeper brewing beneath that pretty façade of hers? Something that may be worth investigating?

Dismissing this last thought, with the remembrance of Dr. Guyton, Jon left to make his own rounds. He would definitely stay committed to his vow and keep his hands off. He didn't need another head case coming after him.

Chapter 5

Dr. Lara Guyton stared out her second floor window at the grounds below. The day was warm and sunny with some of the residents deciding to take advantage of the agreeable weather. She could have joined them, but her thoughts were elsewhere. She was being released.

Lara Guyton, a renowned neurosurgeon, known all over the world for her expert skills in her chosen field, was a transplant to the city from the west coast. After ending a difficult relationship, she thought it was best to make a new start and chose Metro City as the place to do so. Due to their skilled surgical teams, Metro Regional Hospital was one of the highest ranking health facilities in the country, and Lara prided herself in aligning with the best. She had heard only good things about the hospital and its staff, so the choice to become a part of the glory was an easy one. Her brilliant mind would not have allowed her to settle for anything less.

Everyone welcomed her to Metro Regional; beaming with the luck of snagging one of the world's top neurosurgeons. All surgical staff wanted a chance to work with her; to absorb her fresh energy and knowledge, and Jon Payne was no exception.

From the very beginning, she found him intriguing. She would join him in his surgeries to allow him to pick her brain during complicated procedures; techniques that proved useful in sharpening his skills. But soon simple intrigue morphed into shared late night dinners, then breakfast in bed, with Jon seemingly absorbed in every detail of their time together.

Lara loved the attention the handsome doctor poured on her. He was unlike the man from her previous relationship who only worshipped himself. And when she didn't participate in that adoration is when the problems began; problems that had begun to take a toll on her body as well as her mind. Having had enough of the abuse, Lara packed up and moved to Metro City to maintain her reputation and sanity.

Her relationship with Jon was more than she could have anticipated. For the first time ever, she felt valued; not just as a surgeon but as a woman; something she so desperately craved. And even though they agreed upon a non-exclusive pairing, she came to want more; more than what Jon was willing to give. Lara, like so many before her, thought she could change the rules and become his one and only; even to the point of someday becoming his wife. Ultimately, that was her mistake.

To entice him into valuing her more, she started cooking for them instead of eating out or ordering in. She needed Jon to understand there was much more to her than just a scalpel. She was an excellent cook and he agreed after consuming her seductive meals. Meals soon turned into small gifts which soon turned into her showing up unexpectedly at his home. She had become obsessive. Once, when she arrived unannounced, he was entertaining another woman. This is what sent her over the edge. She couldn't believe with all she had done for him, given him, he wanted another after proving there wasn't anyone better suited for him than she.

After Jon refused to see her and started avoiding her at work, Lara became incensed. She watched him give other women attention; attention she felt was hers alone. If she saw him flirting with a nurse, she would make sure that woman's life was hell under her watch. She became so unruly that some of the staff started complaining to the hospital's administrators, who assured they were mistaken. No one wanted to believe a celebrated surgeon, such as Dr. Lara Guyton, was a problem. That was until she tried to stab Dr. Payne. If it hadn't been for his quick reflexes, he could have been seriously injured. His quick thinking only netted him a few bruises from struggling with her on the surgery suite floor. With the help of others in attendance, she was restrained until security was called and she was quickly whisked away. Lara spent the next ten months in a low security facility for the mentally impaired, after Jon refused to press charges. He didn't want to see her in jail. He only asked that she get help.

After she was admitted, it was as if all the life had been drained from her. A thorough examination deemed her deeply depressed; negatively adding to her diagnosed psychosis. A recommendation of required therapy, medication and rest was quickly prescribed. The treatment seemed to have worked. Not only had Lara come to terms with what she had done, but why she had done it. Everything led back to her previous relationship of mental abuse. Her need for mental escape had led to her psychological collapse. When Jon showed her kindness, she had mistaken it to be her salvation. Now she knew better.

Lara had finally come to grips with what she had become due to her obsession with Jon Payne. Every time she thought of her behavior, shame colored her caramel colored cheeks. How could she have been so stupid? So needy? Her actions had been so far out of character she had questioned her own sanity.

She had developed a delusional disorder that had her believing events that weren't quite true. According to her doctor, her acknowledgement of her offenses was the break through that led to her upcoming release. She had faced her problem head on and claimed her unorthodox behavior. With treatment unearthing the cause and ownership of the outburst, the therapist thought it was time for her to rejoin society, but not without limitations.

Her main course of action was to continue her regimen of prescribed medications. However, the one to keep her from returning to the facility or ending up in jail was the directive to stay away from Jon Payne. That meant she would have to look for employment elsewhere. That was fine with her. She couldn't face Jon or any of Metro Regional's staff if she wanted to. Just the thought of the pretend looks of concern and the whispers behind hands, as she left a room, was enough to keep her away.

Resigned to her fate, Lara sighed. It was time she started gathering her things. Her ride would be there shortly to take her home.

Chapter 6

Matthias Bennett eyed his newest colleague James Harrison. The man was a brilliant attorney, but as of late, something didn't seem quite right with him. Matthias was beginning to question his choice in bringing him aboard. It wasn't anything he had or hadn't done. James mastered his craft and was the perfect asset to Bennett Law Group. He was an excellent trial attorney with a high ratio of wins and an all-around good person. So what was it about the man that bothered him?

In fact, James was phenomenal; he couldn't have asked for a better hire. He kept his head down and did his work to near perfection; a trait Bennett was known for. Matthias could even see him as a partner in the firm someday. But outside of his courtroom ability, there seemed to be something simmering just beneath the surface; something Matthias hoped wouldn't suddenly bubble to the top and blow up in his face.

Swiveling in his chair, he asked James to have a seat. "Is everything okay with you James?" He watched him carefully while he waited for an answer.

James's brow furrowed. "Yeah, as far as I know. Why do you ask?" Searching his mind, he hoped he hadn't forgotten something. He may have been somewhat preoccupied, but he prided himself on keeping at least two steps ahead of the game. He hated surprises in any form; feeding into his need to always be aware of every angle at all times. Although he didn't view Matthias's question as a problem—at least not at the moment—still, he liked to be on top of things.

Matthias shook his head. "Nothing. I just know you've had a pretty full workload since you've been here and I just wondered if it might be overwhelming for you, that's all."

James shook his head. "Not in the least. I thrive on pressure. Besides, I like to stay busy. I love this profession. There is nothing like it." He shrugged. "In fact, if I didn't have a load, I wouldn't know what to do with myself." Although James plastered on his most convincing grin, he meant it. If he wasn't working hard, he would be out looking for that bitch Lara who had the nerve to walk out on him.

Satisfied, Matthias nodded. "Just the same, if things get to be too much for you, let me know."

"No problem." James's grin widened. "Is there anything else?

"Yes, how did things go in court yesterday? I know you had a hearing scheduled and your opponent was the new district attorney. Were there any problems?"

James shook his head. "None. The hearing went as planned and I even scored some points with Ms. Ashford." *In more ways than one I might add.*

James's grin spread even wider when he thought of his meeting with the D.A. The woman surprised him. When Jess summoned him for a conference over lunch, he had no idea *his* meat would be served up as the appetizer. The mere thought of that afternoon delight had him wanting to stroke his awakening penis.

"Good to know." Matthias was beginning to think he was wrong about James. Maybe *he* was the one who was over worked. "Keep up the good work." With an acknowledging smile of Matthias' accolades, James left his office and his suspicions.

James Harrison strolled down the corridor to his own office. Things were looking up. He may have lost track of Lara, but he had gained favor with a new playmate, Jess Ashford.

When the new D.A. requested him to join her in her office before the hearing, he assumed it was to discuss his client's case. Although they did discuss the particulars of the case, he soon realized he was there for more than shop talk. He had to hand it to the lady. She knew what she wanted and made no excuses for her choices. After terminating talk of the case, James found himself being serviced by Jess. She went from all business to invading his personal space in a blink of an eye. Before he knew it, she was on her knees firmly and expertly handling his manhood.

He didn't know what to make of her forwardness, but he also wasn't one to complain. If this was how she wanted to conduct business, he was all for it and then some. He, like any other attorney, wasn't above sideline deals. That's what made him good at his craft and bolstered him points in the win column. He had made many under the table deals before, but this one took the cake. He walked out of that office with a better deal than he could have hoped for his client. The man would do some jail time, but nowhere near what he deserved.

James shook his head. He had only been in town for a couple of months and had already made a new influential friend. He couldn't think of anything better than literally being in bed with the district attorney's office. He casually wondered if Ms. Ashford brokered all of her deals with her male opponents in this manner. He hoped not, because he had special plans for her. She would do nicely as a replacement for what he'd lost. He might not have to track down Lara Guyton after all.

Chapter 7

Jon read the text again as he headed to the parking lot; grateful for the reprieve from what would surely be another evening of gunshots and mayhem. He smiled. The text was from Jess.

It was just what he needed coming out of a surgery that was impossible from the beginning. He did his best, but the patient died anyway. He was about to call his brother to see if he wanted to join him for a meal when he saw her message.

He and Jess Ashford had been seeing each other since her first week in town. He had the opportunity to meet her when she sat in on one of her colleague's prepping him for an upcoming trial as an expert witness. He liked her. Unlike Lara, she wasn't a part of the medical field *and* she understood and stuck to the rules.

To break the ice, he invited her to his place for dinner that evening. And for once, he actually cooked instead of ordering takeout. However, instead of easing into the night's foreseen agenda, the moment Jess stepped over the threshold of his home, she was all over him. The woman was insatiable and he liked that most about her. An encounter with her always gave him a run for his money. There was never a dull moment with Metro City's newest district attorney.

Jon chuckled when a text came through from his brother with another plea for an introduction. Landon was hot to know the lady, but there was no way in hell, he was going to let that happen. Besides, even if he wasn't sleeping with Jess, she was far out of Landon's league. His baby brother wouldn't know what to do with an aggressive woman such as Jess Ashford.

With Landon's message forgotten, Jon glanced at his watch before starting his car. According to Jess's timetable, he had just enough time to go home and shower before meeting at her place. One of the other doctors owed him a favor, so the rest of his shift was covered. Tonight he had all the time he wanted to be entertained by Jess.

Lara watched Jon climb into his mint condition, 1968, pearl white Karmann Ghia, from her parked car across the street. She remembered them both tooling around the city in the vintage Volkswagen—his baby. Jon spent a lot of money on that automobile; restoring it inside and out. If she had to guess, that's where his true loyalties lied. He treated that car better and gave it more care than he did any woman he ever dated.

Lara sighed. She had been out of the mental health facility twenty-four hours and was already watching Jon from a parking lot. She honestly didn't know why she was there. Maybe to apologize perhaps? At any rate, she shouldn't be there. Seeing him brought back too many memories that should be left behind. Realizing her mistake, she started the engine and drove away.

James couldn't believe his luck. Sitting across from him, in the lot adjacent to the hospital's parking lot was Lara. One corner of his mouth lifted with glee, as he observed her watching the doctor drive away. He wondered what that was all about. Did she know the man? Better yet, had she slept with him? This latter thought quickly turned his half-hearted smile into rage. When Lara drove from the lot, he followed her. Now that he'd found her, he wasn't about to lose her again.

James wasn't the only one to catch the scene with Lara. Nurse Shelby saw the woman too and she was not happy. Although she knew it wasn't possible for Jon to turn to Lara again, she blamed her for her inability to capture his attention. Through hospital gossip, she recently learned of the incident with Lara, which prompted Jon to never date any woman from the healthcare profession again; and anyone from Metro Regional especially. Lara Guyton had made her task just that more difficult and she despised her for it. One thing was for certain; Shelby had to find a way to make Dr. Jon Payne break his vow of workplace abstinence to be with her.

Chapter 8

Shelby Kirkland, aka Shelby Kane, had made it out of the neighborhood she grew up in by perseverance and hard work. She also had to credit her grandmother Elsa for her constant badgering to do something worthwhile with her life, instead of becoming a part of the current generation of do nothings. After her brother Alonso was lost to the streets, their grandmother wanted to make sure she did not do the same. Most of the girls she grew up with were either single mothers, with little or no education, or a part of the neighborhood's street life. This was a life she quickly realized she didn't want for herself.

After graduating a year early from high school, due to her desire to escape the hood, she legally changed her last name from Kane to Kirkland. She had to rid herself of the stigma of not knowing who she actually belonged to in order to move forward. With her grades, she managed to snag a full ride to college and from there landing a Master's degree in nursing. She promised herself, once she was out of the old neighborhood she would never return, and she hadn't. She had planned to move her grandmother out, but the elderly woman passed away before she could accomplish the task. It was as if she was just waiting to make sure Shelby was safe before taking her spiritual journey home.

Sadly, she never knew her parents, for as long as she could remember, she and her brother lived with their paternal grandmother. Kane—known only by his last name—was a few years older than Shelby, remembered their parents but refused to talk about them. He claimed they weren't worth the trouble. All Shelby had was a name for her father because of their grandmother, who would speak of her son only in hushed tones. It was as if she was afraid to speak of him out loud, as if something bad would happen if she did. And even more peculiar, just like Kane, Elsa wouldn't speak of their mother at all, not even a name. Shelby didn't know if her parents were alive or dead and never knew how she and her brother came to live with their grandmother. It was a mystery Elsa Kane had taken to her grave and Kane took with him when he ran away at seventeen.

Once Shelby graduated grad school, she worked even harder to obtain the available top spot at Metro Regional, the city's most prominent hospital. Transferring from a smaller facility in a neighboring city, she moved back to her home town. Before then, she hadn't been back to Metro City since leaving for college. Even though Shelby had not seen her brother since the day he left their grandmother's, she knew he was still around. Alonso loved Metro City's streets too much to venture anywhere else; streets she knew one day would claim him. She had only been in her position just shy of four months, but each time a gunshot victim came racing through those doors, she held her breath; praying he wasn't one of those on the EMT's gurney in need of emergency care, or worse.

Shelby had spent most of her adulthood cultivating her career, leaving no time for relationships. She rarely dated. But once she met Jon Payne, she vowed to change all of that. She had a mental image of what her dream man would be like, and Dr. Jon Payne fit the bill to a T. And although he saw himself as a forever bachelor, she had other plans. Jon Payne would not only break his vow to date her, but he would make her his wife. She deserved it; she had saved herself for the perfect man and somehow, she would see to it that he would be the one to take the prize.

Chapter 9

Jess Ashford sat in Detective Eric Valero's office. She had a plan to stop the senseless killings on the streets of Metro City. With the mayor's blessing, she was ready to implement it. It wasn't enough to just charge these offenders; it was time to play it tough. She needed the police department to run unexpected but consistent rolling sweeps of the city's crime infested areas. It was time to take down the so-called heads of these warring gangs. Locking up the street level dealers and gangbangers was not enough.

"I need for you to head up this task force and get the ball rolling. The sooner the better. These criminals have to understand this level of crime will not be tolerated in this city." All though she was mentally focused, Jess was staring at Valero's fingers that were currently rubbing his chin, as if she were in a trance. She knew he had his hands full, but from her research, he was the best man for the job. During the former administration's reign of corruption, which included a good chunk of the police department, Valero and his precinct had stayed the course. None of the men and women who served under him were found to be a part of the former mayor's criminal regime. She knew she could trust him.

"Exactly what is it that you have in mind?" He, like every other law abiding citizen, was sick of the nightly gunfights and crime that plagued the city. He agreed. It was time they put an end to it.

"First, you've been authorized to set up a satellite precinct in the heart of the problem area. The building on the corner of Norfolk and Nineteenth Street has been prepared for you and your team to move into. I want you to saturate the streets with your officers in waves."

"Next, pin-point the major players. Target them through their weakest link. There are always those in these gangs who really don't want to be a part of that life, and just need an opportunity to get out. These are the people who are the keys to stopping this madness. I'm working with the feds to give anyone—who is willing to come forward with relevant information—immunity. In addition, we are prepared to offer relocation and witness protection, if necessary. Whatever it takes." Jess was willing to give away the store if it meant cleaning up the streets of Metro City.

"Two questions. First, who's paying for all of this?" Eric liked her plan and it sounded feasible, but it would take a lot more money than what the department's budget could sacrifice for the kind of manpower and overtime she was expecting.

A smile spread over Jess's face. "Why, Wallace and Allen are, of course. The millions of dollars that were seized from their operations are being put to good use. And your second question?"

Eric's lips spread into an easy grin. "When do we get started?"

Jess returned the infectious grin with one of her own.

◄◊►

Jess strutted down the police station's steps, where she was helped into the backseat of her city issued, black Suburban, by her bodyguard and driver, Officer Rafe Santiago, whom she was intimately acquainted. She was pleased with the meeting. And if Detective Valero was half the leader he was reputed to be, they would clean up the streets in no time. She had every faith in him. So much so, she added him to her growing list of potential conquests, as a reward for a job well done.

She glanced up into the rearview mirror at Rafe, whose gaze reluctantly shifted from hers before pulling into traffic. Jess smiled. She had christened him only hours after he was assigned to her security detail. After Rafe had driven her home for the night, she asked him to step inside to make a sweep of her house for any unwanted visitors. When he entered her bedroom, she barred him from leaving until hours later. Even though he was married, Rafe was more than willing to satisfy his new boss and fully agreed with her suggested display of loyalty. Predictably, he made a quick decision that what his wife didn't know wouldn't hurt her.

Shifting her thoughts back to her meeting with the handsome detective, Jess made herself more comfortable on the butter soft leather seat. The meeting she took wasn't just about Metro City's criminals, but also to size up Eric as one of her potential lovers. She had heard a great many things about the detective and one of those being his attractiveness. And her source did not lie. The man was prime; tall, muscular and gorgeous. She could easily place his African American and Hispanic ancestry from his olive skin and regal facial features. She just wondered if he would be a formidable opponent in bed. And if the way he moved was any indication, she was in for a treat.

Her source had also mentioned a girlfriend, but Jess never let that get in the way of what she wanted. Her driver was proof of that. Besides, the girlfriend could have him back once she'd wrung him dry.

As if reading her mind, Rafe glanced once more in the mirror. But this time, Jess didn't return the gesture. He understood his encounter with her was a onetime act, but he couldn't help but wonder what if. The woman was exceptional and he wouldn't have mind one bit for an encore performance.

Chapter 10

Alonso Kane peered around the corner of a burned out building, spying on the young bloods who thought they had taken over his territory. Most on the street never called him by his given name, only his last. He thought it sounded more street worthy than Alonso, with most agreeing.

The disputed territory had become his, after his man Ice had been murdered by the former mayor's rogue cops. And it was time these wannabe thugs understood that. He could have easily delegated the fight and kept a safe distance at his plush spot downtown, but if he was to be a true leader, he needed to be in the trenches with his boys. In his opinion, this was the mistake Ice made when he was running the show.

Once Ice became the head of their corner of the world, he thought he was too good to be out there defending his territory. After all, his aunt was married to the police chief, which in his mind made him better than those under him. According to Ice, the battles were what the street level soldiers were for. As a result, the crew didn't respect him because of his privileged attitude; Kane included. If Ice had been a respected leader, he never would have been in the men's room alone the night that psycho cop pinched him. Ice's boys hadn't cared enough to guard him. Secretly, they all hoped he would disappear off the face of the earth, and Sergeant Riley Phillips had made sure that happened.

It wasn't just Ice's leadership skills that put Kane off, but the way he treated women. Ice handled them as if they were disposable trinkets, meant to be used and tossed away like trash. It was that very behavior that brought about his untimely demise. He misused the cop's girlfriend and he paid for it with his life.

Kane signaled to his men that it was time they taught the young boys a painful lesson. And with that gesture, they descended on the teenaged gangbangers.

He and his crew had quickly rushed those who would take his territory with an unflinching air of superiority. But were soon running for cover when their rivals let go with everything they had, which included rocket launchers and automatic weapons. Unbeknownst to Kane, the teen crew had acquired a cache of high powered weapons just before the take down of Wallace and his bunch. So they were more than prepared for the coming street battle. Out gunned, Kane and his boys retreated in different directions, with a couple of the teens chasing him inside the diner where he was now hiding.

Out of breath, Kane dropped to the floor of the diner before the door closed behind him; only rising slightly to peer out the front window. He couldn't believe it. Those little bastards had some serious fire power.

"What the hell…? Hey! We're closed, so you have got to go!" Trudy stood a few feet away from him with her hands folded on her ample hips. She was just about to lock the door for the night when Kane came rushing inside.

Trying to catch his breath, he waved his gun at her. "Listen lady, just shut your mouth…I ain't got time for this." He was trying to think and he couldn't with Trudy bearing down on him. He had enough trouble with the young bloods outside. He didn't need any hassle from her.

But Trudy didn't back down. "Look, we don't want any trouble, so you need to take *it* and yourself back outside those doors." Pointing, she glared at him. It was bad enough this trash was holding some of the surrounding neighborhoods hostage, she would be damned if he would bring that nonsense inside her diner.

"Lady shut up!" Kane tapped the side of his head with the fist that was closed around his handgun. He had to think.

Ignoring Kane, Trudy turned to the cook, the only other occupant of the restaurant, to call 911, when suddenly there was a deafening, rapid succession of gunfire, with several rounds striking her in the chest. The teens, who were tracking Kane, had sprayed the diner with bullets, killing Trudy instantly.

Feeling confident that they had made their point, the boys took off up the street before someone called the police. Lying prone on the floor with his eyes wide with fear, Kane stared at the fallen woman. His lips trembled. He didn't mean for her to get hurt. He didn't mean for anyone to get caught up in the melee. Unlike some of the other gang leaders, he always managed to protect the innocents from becoming collateral damage. Those people didn't have a dog in their fight.

Shifting his startled gaze from Trudy to the bewildered cook, who was rising from his hiding place behind the counter, Kane swallowed hard before turning his attention to the now bullet shattered window. Seeing no sign of his pursuers, he got to his feet; sliding on broken glass, before bolting out the door in the opposite direction, as the sound of sirens neared the restaurant.

Chapter 11

Jon rolled off of Jess just as both of their phones began to vibrate and buzz. He squinted at the clock and groaned. With the late hour that could only mean one thing. He was needed at the hospital. At least he had gotten in a few hours of playtime with his favorite lady D.A.

They had spent the evening enjoying each other in every imaginable position with a few he thought weren't possible. Jon loved Jess's drive to try any and everything. There wasn't anything he could come up with that she wasn't willing to explore. Jess Ashford was an exceptional woman and she knew it. Most men would feel threatened by her self-confidence, but for him, it was an instant turn on.

Jess sat up to answer her phone. She listened intently while the caller filled her in. Among the other gunshot victims of the night, there had been a shooting at a restaurant, leaving an elderly woman dead. She slowly released the breath she was holding. It was bad enough when the animals killed each other, but when the carnage spilled over into everyday citizens' lives, it was unforgiveable. She hoped Detective Valero was ready, because they were about to steam roll over the criminal element starting now. Clicking off her phone she turned to Jon.

With his lips pressed together, he shook his head. "Before you say it, I know you have to go. So do I. There are more bodies to patch up." Jon sighed. He was sick of the carnage too. But at the moment, he was irritated because his time with Jess had been interrupted.

She leaned in to taste his lips. "Don't worry. It won't be long before this nonsense will end and you and I will have more free time than we'll know what to do with." Jess caressed his cheek with the back of her hand. If she was into feelings and relationships, Jon would be a top contender. But neither one of them wanted or needed that. She especially didn't. Variety was more to her liking than being tied to one man. It could never work for them.

She tried swinging her legs over the side of the bed, but before she could, Jon pulled her back into his arms.

"We have time for a quickie." And without waiting for her protest, he pulled her under him and entered her; taking her fast and hard.

Chapter12

While surveying the mess in the diner, Detective Valero used his clinched jaw to suppress his anger. He recognized Trudy Franklin immediately. She was the regulars' favorite waitress. But what most didn't know, Trudy was not just the establishment's beloved mother figure, but its owner, with him being one of the few people who knew. Eric was beyond livid.

Trudy Franklin was a good friend, so he always made it a point to direct the new hires to her place for a good meal. Her warm humor, along with the great food, made the diner the department's unofficial eatery. Any given time there would be at least one officer, on or off duty, patronizing the place—except for tonight. Eric shook his head with regret, but didn't bother to play the 'if only' game with himself. He knew it was pointless. There was no way possible this tragedy could have been predicted.

Trudy opened the diner nearly forty years' prior with only a few dollars and a dream; quickly turning it into the city's place to be. People from all walks of life frequented *Randy's Place*. The draw was the good southern cooking and even better hospitality. With the diner's popularity, Trudy could have easily sold it and lived the high life for the rest of her days. He often teased her about cashing in and living it up in France or somewhere equally glamorous. But she said her only dream was to make people happy and living in luxury on foreign soil, with any amount of money, wasn't going to do that for her.

Trudy loved the people of Metro City. And besides supplying its citizens with great food, she gave back by anonymously sponsoring a substantial scholarship through the police department; awarded during their annual Christmas party. Eric had been honored when she chose him to present the much desired funds to a deserving candidate each year. During the summer, she made it a point to hire teens from the neighborhood to work at the diner for extra pocket money. She knew some of the single parents had a difficult time and wanted to lend a helping hand wherever she could.

Eric swiped a hand down his face. Now Trudy was dead with all of her hopes and dreams for the community snuffed out with her; all because some disrespectful assholes thought nothing of her life.

Turning, he watched one of his men assist in helping the witness with his timeline of events. From what he gathered from Roscoe, Trudy's head cook, one of the bangers had run inside the restaurant just as they were closing. But before he could dial for help, the place exploded with bullets. From the cook's description, the banger sounded a lot like Alonso Kane, one of the people who were at the top of his list of future arrests. Now he had an even greater reason to shut him and his crew down for good.

"So what do we have here?" This was Jess. She accessed the room as she picked her way carefully through the broken shards of glass. As head prosecutor, she wasn't required to come out to crime scenes, but if she was going to make her plan a success, she needed to put a face on it and to see it through from start to finish. She wanted everyone to know she was in it for the long haul.

Eric nodded in the direction of Trudy's body on the floor. "According to the witness, Trudy here confronted a banger who rushed into the diner armed. She was in the process of throwing him out when all hell broke loose. Two more bangers," he pointed in the direction of the street, "presumed rivals, stood just outside… opening fire without cause." He paused, before continuing, "Killing her, but missing their intended target, who Roscoe says fled immediately after they left."

"I want boots on the ground starting from this point on. We must answer this madness with a swift and complete lock down of the surrounding neighborhoods. It's time for this to end!" Jess was angry. She, like most on the scene, had met Trudy and liked her instantly.

"I'm already ahead of you. Every available cop in the city and some from surrounding townships are swarming through the streets as we speak. I expect to have who's responsible by dawn," Eric informed her.

Eric and Jess both turned at quickening footsteps heading in their direction. It was one of Eric's officers making his way toward them.

"Detective, what—?" Landon never finished his sentence before spotting Trudy's lifeless body lying amid the rubble on the floor. He was on the other side of town when the call came through that there was gunfire at the diner. He had broken the sound barrier trying to get there to see about Trudy. Landon was beside himself. He couldn't fathom who would want to kill someone who was as sweet and kind as Trudy Franklin.

Witnessing Landon's distress, Eric let him have a moment before he spoke. Landon was finding it difficult to tear his eyes and heart away from his slain friend. He felt the young officer's pain, but they had a job to do.

"Officer, I know this is difficult, but we need every able body out in this community to find who is responsible for this."

Landon, struggling to get his emotions in check, nodded. "Yes sir." He turned on his heels to hit the streets.

Sympathizing with Landon's distress, Jess spoke up. "Officer. Did you know Ms. Franklin well?"

He turned back and nodded again. "Yes, I did. That woman couldn't have been any better to me if she were my own mother." He shrugged. "She sort of took me under her wing and whenever I was assigned to this district, I made it a point to stop by to make sure she was okay." Landon felt if he had been patrolling the area tonight Trudy would still be alive.

"Come by my office after your shift. I want to get some insight on Ms. Franklin and the people who frequented the diner. And since you are a regular, you may know something that can help this case," Jess told him.

Landon nodded a final time at them both, before heading back to his squad car.

Eric peered through the shattered window after him. He had been keeping an eye on him for a while now. Landon Payne may have only been on the force for a short period of time, but he had already racked up several commendations. He had foiled and solved crimes that were usually handled by seasoned detectives. With Landon's natural skills and instincts, Eric felt he would make a good detective. And once the city was back to a quieter pace, he would make certain that his promotion happened.

Jess also watched Landon make his way back outside. She had seen him before and knew exactly who he was—Jon Payne's younger brother. She had already added him to her wish list awhile back, after she and Jon started sleeping together. It didn't bother her one bit that the two were brothers. Jess had been with related men before; sometimes at the same time. And if the Payne brothers were game, she would gladly agree to a threesome.

She gave her attention to Landon until he was no longer visible. She would gauge his readiness for her later.

Chapter 13

True to his word, the perpetrators of Trudy's murder were sitting in separate interrogation rooms at MCPD headquarters. All Eric could do at the moment was to stare at the pair via video screens. He couldn't believe how young they were. They were babies, barely teenagers. But what got to him the most was their unresponsiveness and lack of remorse for what they had done. They had taken a life and it didn't seem to faze them in the least. They couldn't have cared less that an innocent soul had fallen due to their rampage.

Jess's jaw dropped when she entered the room and spotted the pair. "These babies are what's been terrorizing Metro City?" She blinked; believing her eyes were playing tricks on her. She was expecting seasoned, hardened criminals not these children.

Eric sighed deeply. "I'm afraid so."

Recovering from her initial shock, Jess shook her head in indifference. She would not be moved by their ages. "It doesn't matter. I plan to charge them and ask for the maximum sentence possible just as if they were grown ass men. Maybe it'll shake-up the rest of these baby wannabe's."

Any other time Eric would have disagreed and argued the point that they could be saved, but looking into these boys' eyes, there was nothing there. They were dealing with soulless sociopaths and there was no cure for that. They needed to be locked away from decent society.

They both turned from the boys when they heard the door open. Eric grinned. It was his girlfriend KT Ellis. Her presence brought a much needed distraction from a dismal situation. And if things went according to plan, he would be asking her to become his wife in a couple of days. He had everything planned out; from the perfect ring, to the proposal venue. He couldn't wait. His grin widened.

"Hey baby, what are you doing here?" He kissed her when she reached him.

"I heard about last night and Trudy." KT also knew the lovable woman and would miss her.

"Babe have you met D.A. Ashford?" KT shook her head; turning to face Jess.

"Hi, KT Ellis." She extended her hand to Jess.

Plastering on a counterfeit smile, Jess reached out to limply grasp KT's fingertips, as if touching her was undesirable. Although KT was taken aback by the woman's actions, she didn't let it show.

"Jess, KT here is a lead investigator with Hudson and Associates. But what I'm most proud of is this beauty is my lady." Eric leaned into KT for another kiss from her tinted lips.

After the show of affection, KT turned back to Jess, but not before wrapping both arms around one of Eric's bulging biceps; pulling him closer to her side. A gesture not missed by Jess or Eric, who hid a small smile. He didn't know exactly what was going on, but he was sure to hear about it later.

"Nice to finally meet you. I've heard nothing but good things from my boss. Tor admires what you're trying to accomplish. And if there is anything that we can do to help you in your fight to clean up Metro City, please let us know." KT had plastered on her own smile, but hers was much more convincing than Jess's.

"I'll be sure to do that," Jess answered sweetly. Even though she was acquainted with Tor Hudson and his operation, and counted him as an ally, she doubted if she would be calling on him. That would mean she would have to look up in this heffa's face again. Something she did not care to do.

Jess distastefully eyed KT a final time, before shifting her gaze back to Eric. "I will check in with you later to go over plans for these two," she told him; motioning toward the two teen murder suspects. Eric nodded.

And I'll be checking up on you too sweetie, KT thought, as the phony woman left the room. Tor may have had good things to say, but she would bet her last dollar there were some not so good things this woman was hiding.

Chapter 14

Jess was furious by the time she made it back to her office. It took everything inside of her not to slam her door. With that woman watching over her prey like some overprotective rabid dog, there was no way she was going to be able to get close to Eric Valero. She wasn't fooled by KT's sugary sweet smile either. Her lips may have said happy, but her eyes said 'I'm watching you bitch'. She would have to do a little investigating of her own to see just who this KT person was and what she was up against. Jess was not to be out done and she wasn't giving up on Eric unless she was absolutely forced too.

KT's awareness of her wasn't the only thing that had upset her. KT Ellis's presence was overwhelming, with the perfect slim build and her cute little pixie haircut. And to top it off, she and Eric Valero made the perfect couple without even trying. Jess hated women like her. Everything came so easily for them.

Jess Ashford was pretty in her own right with plump rounded curves that most men considered vivacious, but some women considered dumpy, because of her short stature. Unlike the long legged woman who stood in the way of her goal. And whereas KT displayed perfect skin, Jess had to work hard to contain the acne that pledged her most of her life with a cabinet full of lotions and creams to prove it.

Turning at a knock on her door, she asked the visitor to come inside while she settled herself at her desk. It was Landon Payne. This time Jess's smile was genuine. She had forgotten she had asked him to stop by, but was glad to see him all the same. He was just what she needed to take her mind off of KT Ellis—at least for now.

Grinning like a well satiated cat, Jess stretched out naked across her bed, letting the intricately designed ceiling fan cool her warm skin. She was fresh from the shower, where the warm, steady stream from her handheld showerhead brought her to another completed climax. She used the pulsating water to satisfy the fantasy of Landon sharing the bath with her. Her body continued to hum, as she lay amid the disheveled sheets; savoring the still present masculine scent that brought to mind the presence of his body atop hers. Pressing her knees together, she recalled the feel of him inside her. The decision to engage Landon Payne was a brilliant one.

After speaking with Landon, about Trudy and some of the other regular customers, she invited him back to her place for breakfast. They both had been up all night and hadn't had a moment to eat. Landon was hesitant at first, but it hadn't taken but a small nudge and a promise of a home cooked country breakfast to persuade him into accepting.

She cooked and they ate as promised. Jess prepared most of what she discovered were Landon's favorites. They ate eggs over easy, pancakes, grits and an entire package of perfectly cured bacon. During their meal, she asked him questions to get to know him better, with him asking her guided personal questions, to which she opted to show him the answers rather than tell. Before Landon knew what hit him, Jess had undressed them both and led him to her bedroom.

Thinking she would have to bark orders at the seemingly inexperienced man, she was pleasantly surprised when he took charge from the beginning. Jon Payne's not so little brother had her whimpering and howling as if she were a novice. She couldn't believe the man's prowess. He had a unique way of handling her and she loved every moment of him. The feel of him inside her body was unlike anything she could recall in her previous encounters. He knew the right amount of pressure and thrust to send her over the edge multiple times. And the tempo he set was different every time. Landon Payne was unique in every way imaginable, and it pleased her to no end.

There were several marked differences between Landon and Jon and the differences were all in Landon's favor. Big brother couldn't hold a candle to Landon's penis length or girth which was just the tip of the iceberg. In regards to its silky texture, Landon was magnificent. She could have held him in her mouth for days. And where as she had to prod Jon into rough trade, Landon took to it like a duck to water. He was by no means new to the game. He was stern right up to the edge, but not once crossing that thin invisible line. Teasing her breasts and inner thighs with tiny pin pricks inflicted by his teeth that left welts to signify that he had been there.

After experiencing Landon, Jess thought it was time to trade up and bid his brother farewell. She even decided to cut James Harrison loose *and* give up her power play for Detective Valero. Let that she-wolf bitch have Valero, she had found the perfect one.

Chapter 15

Landon lay in his bed staring up at the ceiling. He should have been wiped out, but he felt as if he could run for miles. It was early evening when he'd showered and slipped nude between the cool sheets to grab a few hours of sleep before starting his shift. He was still wired; and thoughts of his afternoon with Jess weren't helping. He found his body hadn't forgotten her either. He absently lowered his hand to his groin to manage the generous erection that had materialized there. Jess had that effect on him.

Breakfast had been more than he could have ever hoped for. He hadn't known what she had in mind when she invited him to her place. He thought they would just continue their discussion about Trudy and all the other crimes that were threatening to take over the city. He may have been surprised by Jess's aggression, but he wasn't about to let that forfeit the opportunity to be with her. Here he was badgering his brother about an introduction when it took the woman herself to make the first move.

The thought of Jon brought with it a chuckle. His brother made a sport of collecting women for his ever present carnal desires, only to discard them when they wanted more than a causal connection. When the women became too clingy, he would just move on to the next conquest. It was rumored that Jon had entertained at least ten different women in just that year alone. Landon shook his head at his brother's passive lifestyle. He wondered what Jon would think of him laying claim to the one woman with whom he had not been successful. He felt the only reason he avoided introducing him to Jess was that he himself had failed to close the deal. And knowing his brother, this didn't sit to well with his ego.

Jess Ashford was by all accounts a challenge; a woman deeper and sharper than those Jon normally engaged. He could understand why his big brother's shallow behavior didn't move her. The woman was fierce. Even he had to admit, Jess had been a little intimidating, although it didn't stop him from following her lead. However, once he understood his role, he pushed any hesitation aside to take charge; leaving her agreeably intrigued and surrendering to his proof that he was worthy of the offered position.

Jess made him feel like a NASCAR driver as he drove over and into every curve of her body to completion. He handled the lady D.A. firmly; applying the correct amount of skill and performance that left no doubt that he was more than up for the task and she adored every moment of it. He didn't think twice about manhandling her. He instinctively knew she was down for whatever he threw at her, with her managing every thrust and expertly controlled punishment accordingly. And when he finally allowed himself to succumb to her dominance, it took superhuman strength to stop himself from releasing when she placed him inside her mouth and swallowed him whole. That was no small feat. Landon knew he was a big boy with no one ever accomplishing that task before.

Although he wanted to see her again, Landon hadn't allowed himself to hope for more than that afternoon. Unlike his brother, he had always been a one-woman man, but the lady was in the driver's seat. Because she had initiated their tryst, he felt he had no right to make any unwarranted suggestions and she hadn't offered any. If he could have his way, Jess Ashford would be a permanent fixture in his life. His misgivings were soon laid to rest with the chime of his mobile phone. He had just turned into his driveway when Siri informed him that Jess wanted to see him again. He grinned when he recalled her message: "You're a keeper. See you soon."

Landon was starting to feel the effects of the day's pleasurable workout. Knowing he needed to sleep, he gave into the involuntary closing of his eyelids. His body was finally demanding rest before starting his extended tour of duty. Tired as he was, he didn't mind grabbing the voluntary overtime. They may have captured Trudy's killers, but the department still needed to maintain the strong presence they had in the community. No one wanted a repeat of last night's tragedy.

This thought brought him back to the night before. He would never see the lovable woman again. It seemed as if he'd known Trudy his entire life. He couldn't remember a time when she wasn't present. She was gone because of senseless madness. He rolled over onto his left side and released an unsteady breath. He would miss the woman who was like a second mother to him. Metro City wouldn't be the same without her.

Though his thoughts were still on Trudy, he soon drifted into a deep slumber. His body needed replenishing, if his mind did not.

Chapter 16

Jess yawned as she sluggishly made her way toward the pounding on her front door. It was two o'clock in the morning and some idiot was trying to wake the entire neighborhood. She tightened the belt to her robe, as she shuffled down the dimly lit hallway to give the late night visitor a piece of her mind. Checking the peephole, she found it was a uniformed Landon on the other side. She quickly released the latch and threw open the door.

"Landon, what—" Jess started.

"Are you alright?" Landon gave her a cursory sweep before advancing hurriedly inside the house.

"Landon, what the hell is going on?!" Jess folded her arms while he moved swiftly from room to room, with her hot on his heels demanding an answer.

"We got a call from one of your neighbors. She thought she saw someone prowling around outside your house." Jess continued to follow him throughout the house, while he checked every window and door.

Satisfied that everything was secure, he turned to gauge her reaction. "I've already checked outside; did you hear anything?"

She frowned. "No, I was asleep until I heard you banging."

"Jess you have to be careful. You may have only been in town a short while, but you have made some powerful enemies since implementing your prosecuting policies. There are a lot of people who want to see you hurt or worse.

She raked her fingers through her silky brown hair, before heading back to her bedroom with Landon following. She shrugged. "It comes with the territory," she added nonchalantly.

"Look, you can't think that way. This is no game. These fools out here are playing for keeps. This person may not have done anything this time, but what about the next time? The last prosecutor, who had his life threatened, woke up to a burning house and *he* was taking the threats seriously."

Landon pulled her into his arms. He didn't know what he would do if something happened to her. He kissed the top of her head. Drawing her closer, he slid his large hands from her back to her generously rounded behind; pressing himself against her. She may have had his heart racing with the thought of what could have happened to her, but he also found it a turn on to be her rescuer.

Seeing where this was leading, Jess untied her robe and let it fall to the floor, exposing her nude body. Landon's breathing increased as he cupped her full breasts. Moaning, he reluctantly let go of her to remove his gun belt; placing it on a nearby chair. Jess's breath caught when he returned to suck a nipple into his mouth while she released his trousers and underwear to pool around his ankles.

With this task completed, Landon took charge, turning her to bend her over the dresser; entering her swiftly as she moaned for mercy. After he came, Jess fell to her knees, placing his now semi-flaccid penis into her mouth to clean him up. With Landon, she wasn't usually satisfied with a quickie, but he was on duty. It wouldn't bear well if he was out of touch for too long. It might prompt someone to come looking for him. And neither one of them could afford that.

Pulling her to her feet, Landon kissed her before pulling up his shorts and trousers and replacing his belt. It was time that he left. This would be the first of many late night calls to Jess's. Every night he was on duty, he would make it a point to sneak away to her home to protect and service her.

Landon was so busy attending to Jess that neither one of them noticed the shadow that hurried from the sparsely covered window. Jess, assuming her bedroom was secure from prying eyes, because of the privacy fence, had left the blinds partially open. Getting what he needed, the intruder let himself out through the unlocked side gate to hurry to his parked car a few yards down the street. He couldn't believe his luck. He almost didn't leave his car once the police car swung into the driveway. But acting a hunch, he decided to see for himself what was going on at the prosecutor's home.

After quietly positioning himself at Jess's bedroom window, he captured a full ten minutes of video of the two on his iPhone. His employer would be pleased.

James Harrison angrily took a long swallow of his beer, nearly draining the bottle. He was hoping to catch that cow in the act after she dumped him. But when he peered into her window it was pitch dark and he couldn't even make out if anyone was in Jess's bed, let alone if she was sleeping alone. He had only been there a few minutes when the next door neighbor's backyard light came one. He took it as his cue to leave. It wouldn't have been wise to linger only to be caught stalking Metro City's prosecutor. There was no way to explain his presence.

Clutching the now empty bottle, he barely controlled the urge to throw it across the room. He was beyond agitated. Just when he was about to get settled in for a long and enjoyable stint with Jess as his starring witness, the bitch dumps him. What angered him the most, she gave him no explanation. That could only mean there was another man involved.

This was the second woman who kicked him to the curb in a short period of time, and he wasn't, by any stretch of imagination, going to forget it any time soon. First that ungrateful cow Lara skipped town on him and now the D.A. thought she could pull a fast one. He must be slipping, because women didn't walk away from him *ever*. He used them until *he* was finished, not the other way around. He'd had enough of these disobedient females and somebody needed to pay and pay soon.

But first, he needed to find out who the lady prosecutor dropped him for. It might benefit him to take that route instead of taking his revenge out on Jess directly.

If the guy was easily influenced, he may be able to intimidate him into abandoning his claim. But in the meantime, he needed to keep a closer eye on his ex. That bitch had to pay for sure.

Chapter 17

Jon sat at his desk rubbing his eyes. It had been another long shift and he was tired. He wanted to go home, but he received a text from Jess stating she was in the building and needed to see him. Even though he hadn't seen her in a few days, he hoped the visit wasn't for any quick play; as tired as he was, he didn't think he could accommodate her. Yawning, he cut it short at the knock at his door.

"Come in."

Jon, leaning forward in his chair, had closed his eyes to massage away a knot of tension that had settled itself at the base of his neck. When he opened them, it wasn't Jess who stood before him, but Lara Guyton. He bolted upright in his chair not sure what to expect. His eyes cut quickly to the phone on his desk. It would just have to do if things got out of hand, since she stood between him and the door. Lara saw the move and pressed her lips together. Despite Jon's unease, she moved closer to stand directly in front of his desk.

"Jon, you can relax, I didn't come here to cause trouble. I just wanted to let you know that I released and to tell you how sorry I am for everything I've done. I have no excuses…there is no excuse. My behavior was, well…unacceptable. Not only had I put you in an awkward position, but the hospital as well, which makes it impossible for me to continue to be a part of the staff here. So you don't have to worry, after today you will never see me again. I've put in for a transfer to another hospital in another state. It will be a fresh start from this madness for the both of us." She laughed at this last statement; hoping it would ease some of the tension in the room.

Although she chuckled at her play on words, Lara Guyton stood ramrod straight; clenching and unclenching her hands into tight angry fists, which were currently hidden behind her back. The manic gesture was clearly warring with the calm façade she was displaying to Jon. At the beginning of her speech, she had splayed both hands on the surface of his desk. She needed him to understand that she was not there to harm him; hoping he would accept the apology without question. It was important that he believed her.

Jon's tensed shoulders visibly relaxed. He was relieved to hear she wasn't there to do any further damage.

In his opinion, she had done quite enough. But even though the woman had tried to kill him, he didn't feel any real animosity towards her. He had experienced angry confrontations from women before. Although this one was the most serious, he felt he may have played a small part in her breakdown. He saw her slipping way long before he tried breaking things off with her and should have addressed the situation then, instead of turning a blind eye. Maybe if he had, the situation wouldn't have gotten as far as it did.

As twisted as it was, when she started coming off the rails, a small part of him found pride in her overdramatic reaction to him. Lara wasn't just another female who wanted him. She was an influential figure, who had lost her composure over a man; lost it over him, and the knowledge of this boosted his ego. But after the episode in the O.R., he had enough sense to check his ego at the door from that point on. Having someone attempt to stab you to death with a scalpel brought reality back home without hesitation.

He settled back into his chair; slightly rocking as he considered her. Sitting forward once more, he finally spoke. "Lara, I accept your apology and wish you all the best. And forgive me *if* I contributed in any way to what happened."

If? What an arrogant bastard.

Even though Jon hadn't placed an emphasis on the word, Lara's mind chose to interpret it otherwise. Her fists clenched and unclenched tighter and faster, as she considered this. Deciding to take the high road, she shook her head.

"It wasn't anything you did," she lied. "We both laid the ground rules up front and I should not have had any expectations of them changing." Her hands relaxed behind her back. He did accept her apology, and that was the whole purpose of her being there.

When he opened his mouth to say more, she shook her head to stop him. She really didn't need or want to hear anything more from him. She had a task to fulfill and she needed to finish with as little input from him as possible. This was her show not his.

She continued her reassurance. "Jon, you did nothing wrong. You were just being…yourself," she informed him with a gesture of her hands, which had relaxed enough to be visible. "It was my mistake. If I couldn't handle your boorish approach in dealing with women, I should have excused myself from the situation, or better yet, not engaged at all. I knew your reputation, and I should have never stuck my hand in the fire, knowing there was a great chance I could have it burned off if I didn't remove it soon enough." She finished with a small, tight smile; the equivalent of the fists that had suddenly returned to their hiding place.

Jon's eyes narrowed at her veiled diatribe. If this was an apology, why did he feel as if he had been insulted? But before he could mull this over further, Lara spoke again.

"Well, that's all I came to say. I'm packing up and should be gone by the end of next week. You take care of yourself Jon Payne." After another small smile, she let herself out of his office.

For a long while, Jon sat staring at the closed door. "What the hell did she mean, I was just being myself? Boorish? Hand in the fire...what the—"

Once again, his opportunity to analyze her words was interrupted by a second knock at his door. This time it had to be Jess. But instead of asking the visitor to come in, he quickly moved around his desk to answer the door himself. If there was another unwanted person there, he would stop them before they entered his office to create more confusion.

He grinned when he opened the door to his expected guest. Stepping aside, he allowed her entrance before closing and locking the door behind him. After Lara's strange visit, he suddenly acquired a fresh burst of energy; making him ready and willing to participate in whatever Jess had in mind. Moving to stand in front of her, he stroked her shoulders as he attempted to kiss her, only to be gently, but undeniably rebuffed.

Jon's smile disappeared. *What the hell is going on this morning? One woman insults me and now this one is cold-shouldering me?*

Side stepping his amorous advances, Jess set the tone for her visit by taking a seat in the armed chair near his desk; preventing any further physical contact. Taking her cue, he reclaimed his seat with the tangible and intangible barrier separating them.

"We need to talk," Jess started. She wasn't in the mood for unnecessary small talk.

Jon frowned. Whenever *he* started a conversation with 'we need to talk', he was about to dump someone. This awareness brought a deeper frown.

"About…?" He let the sentence hang, because he had a feeling he knew where this was headed.

Jess sighed before she spoke. "Jon, it's been fun, but it's time that I moved on." She paused to let that sink in. If Jon was the man he insisted he was, she wouldn't have to go any further by offering explanations.

They both knew it wouldn't last, and yes, it may be ending sooner than they both expected, but he just wasn't his brother. In fact, she had already dismissed her other playmates, in order to be with Landon exclusively; something she had never done before. She didn't know how long her fling with him would last, but she was ready for the long haul and hoped he was too. She would discuss it with him tonight when he made his scheduled 'protect and serve' visit. She couldn't wait. Landon never disappointed her. She smiled at the thought.

For the second time that morning, Jon narrowed his eyes at a smiling woman. Did everyone have it in for him today? But one thing was for sure, Jess had found herself another playmate and he meant enough for her to drop him without a moment's notice. For once, Jon Payne was on the receiving end of a dismissal and he didn't like it one bit. His frown deepened.

Gathering himself, he spoke, "Ok, is that all?" His attitude may have appeared resigned, but he was anything but. He was furious.

Accepting he was in agreement, Jess's smile widened in relief. He really was the man he claimed to be. She loved how her endings were no muss, no fuss. Although she didn't think he would resist, she was always at the ready when she handed a man his walking papers. She fully understood men and their egos and how delicate they could be, but she always managed to walk the fine line between mutual agreement and trouble. She never had a problem in all the years she'd played the game, but there was always a first time for everything. She was grateful Jon wasn't it.

Standing to her feet, she nodded. "That's it." She blew him a parting kiss before exiting his office for good.

"No, that is not it!" Jon ground out his displeasure through clenched teeth. He wanted to know how this could happen to him. But most importantly, who had replaced him and what did the new man have that he didn't?

Dr. Jon Payne had gotten a taste of his own medicine and it was bitter.

Chapter 18

Lara sat at her vanity staring into the oversized mirror, vacantly twirling a lock of her hair around her index finger. She didn't notice the disheveled image reflecting back at her. The one that displayed unkempt hair, shadowed eyes from lack of sleep and cracked lips. She wasn't looking at herself, but back in the past where she and Jon were happy.

It had only been three weeks after her release, but she had stopped taking her medication long before she left the institution. In her mind, she didn't need them anymore. She told herself what happened with Jon could never repeat itself, because her intelligence and will power was far greater than any fleeting mental issue she may have haphazardly fell into. She didn't have a problem. But the more time lapsed, the more unstable she became; but never enough to miss her weekly sessions with her outpatient physician. Somehow, she was always able to pull herself together just enough to fool the man. However, she had enough mental capacity to realize the oversight was due to his interest in her. The therapist couldn't have cared less if she slipped a little, as long as he could take a peek under the short skirts that always included the nonexistent underwear she managed to forget to don each session.

Lara didn't mind the horny man's anxious visual probing and impressive hard-on, as long as he kept writing those positive reports each week. And if at some point, it required her to lift one of those short skirts and climb onto his lap for a ride, she would do that too; anything to prevent her from being locked up again away from Jon Payne.

Although she told Jon he wouldn't see her again after her last visit, her declaration didn't include her not seeing him. She was there most mornings sitting in her car at the end of his shifts just to watch him walk across the parking lot. She marveled how he could stroll along so full of himself; without a care in the world after wrecking her life. The more she watched him the angrier she became.

Lara's small smile had widened once she left Jon's office. She caught the display of uncertainty that flashed across his face when she was giving her 'apology'. She had hit a nerve. She thought this jab would have been satisfying, but after mulling over her situation, along with her system free of medication, she accepted that she wasn't the blame for what happened between them. Jon Payne was a class A asshole who deserved every stab of her scalpel had she been successful. What made him think he could screw around with her and drop her when *he* got ready? She was sick of men using her. Between Jon and her ex James, she didn't know who was worst. But after thoroughly comparing the two, decidedly, she came to the conclusion Jon Payne was far worse.

James Harrison may have inflicted pain on her body sexually, but it was nothing compared to how Jon played with her heart. He made her feel as if she had a chance at a normal relationship; one where there was love and kindness. She recalled how they would spend time together talking of a future that included children. She told him how much she adored them and planned to have as many as she could stand someday. She even asked him if he wanted children and he said yes. She knew that it was true because of how he interacted with them whenever they came into the ER; how he gave them fatherly attention. She had even complimented him on his natural paternal instinct; accolades he readily accepted.

Unlike Jon, James never wanted children; always citing how they were an unnecessary nuisance he couldn't stomach. James may have been cruel, but he never led her to believe any more than what he gave her. There were no surprises there. She knew what he was about from the beginning and he never let her forget it. But James was comfortable, someone to come home to; and at the time that was all she required. They probably would have still been together if it had not been for her inability to endure his warped view of love making. Only after she experienced Jon's warmth and tenderness, did she become fully aware of just how cruel James had been. Where Jon provided comfort, James meted out pain and degradation.

Lara met James at an upscale sex club she occasionally visited. Anytime she became particularly bored with her life, she visited the club for some excitement, by choosing a willing partner for the night. She had been there several times before spotting him at the bar, seemingly unimpressed with the small group of females who were unsuccessfully vying for his attention. Feeling she had nothing to lose, she sat beside him and struck up a conversation. They discovered they had other things in common beyond the club scene. Soon they started meeting outside the club, which eventually led to them moving in together.

It was fun and games at first, but in the end, James's sadism became more than she bargained for or could bear; leaving her no alternative but to leave him. She knew James would have made it impossible to end the relationship without some sort of confrontation, so she packed up her things and left without notice. It was time she reclaimed herself.

When she landed in Metro City and joined the hospital staff, her emotions were fragile but mending. And with the help of Jon Payne, came the understanding of what she truly needed—love. But instead of healing her, he took her tender soul and nursed it back to health, until he was tired of her. He left her free-falling into madness, without so much as a visit or a phone call while she was institutionalized. He never cared for her, only pretended to.

Lara continued to twirl her hair while concluding that Dr. Payne needed a lesson in compassion and she was just the woman to teach him. She wasn't going anywhere until Jon understood how real pain felt.

Chapter 19

Hurriedly driving from Jess's neighborhood, Jon's heart beat so hard and fast he thought it would pound its way out of his chest. Never in a million years could he have foreseen what he witnessed tonight.

When he pulled up to the curb at Jess's house, there was a patrol car parked in her driveway. He'd heard about the trouble she'd had with someone prowling around outside her home, so his curiosity was piqued the moment he spotted the police car. He hoped she was alright. Even though she'd dumped him, he was still concerned. But concern wasn't what brought him to her house tonight. It was his burning need to know who had replaced him in her bed.

It bothered him how she dropped him so abruptly, usually that was his M.O. But when he found himself on the receiving end of things, it troubled him more than he cared to admit or had a right to be. But he had to know the identity of the man who replaced him so deftly, that he never saw it coming.

Leaving his car, Jon took his time reaching her door. Only giving the squad car a brief glance as he passed it, his sole focus was on Jess. He was about to ring the bell but hesitated. Should he even be there? He checked his watch. It was a little past one in the morning. How would he explain his presence at her home this late at night? Decidedly not caring about explanations, he reached for the bell again, but found himself trying the door handle instead.

Hoping against hope, he pressed the lever to find the door unlocked. Slowly pushing it open, it never occurred to him, by walking into her home unannounced, the cop inside could mistake him for an intruder and shoot him. And it certainly never dawned on him that the police visit could be a personal one, even though there wasn't a single light on that could be seen from the street. His unreasoning mind wouldn't allow him to think that far ahead.

Dismissing all the warning signs that this was a bad idea, Jon stepped forward inside the foyer, quietly closing the door behind him. He had one final moment when a small voice of reason tried to dissuade him from his foolhardy task, but he shut it down as quickly as it came. Silently picking his way through the dimly lit house, he followed the unmistakable sounds of someone making love, until he reached Jess's bedroom. Instead of stopping himself and retracing his steps back to his car, Jon propelled himself forward to finally learn the mystery man's identity. Hesitant, he came to a complete stop just inside the doorway where all the lights were on.

Jon took in the complete performance in one clear viewing; the position of Jess's body; the satiated sneer of ecstasy unmistakably blooming on her face; and the hand that held a fist full of Jess's thick disheveled hair. But what fully captured his attention was the hand that held the hair. He allowed his gaze to travel from the large, long fingered hand up the arm until it landed on Landon's distorted face, as he grunted and pounded into Jess's bare, up turned lower half.

"What the hell is going on here?!" Jon wanted to denounce his seemingly lying eyes, but he couldn't deny what lay before him. His little brother was manhandling Jess and she was enjoying every brutal moment of it.

At the sound of Jon's outraged voice, Landon and Jess both stopped in mid stroke, with Landon quickly pulling out of her with a wet smacking sound, leaving him stumbling over his pants and briefs pooled around his ankles.

Catching his balance, a startled Landon, questioned his brother. "What the…Jon what the hell are you doing here?"

"What…? Me?" Jon didn't know what to address first. His surprised gaze quickly swung from Jess to Landon and back to Jess again. He couldn't believe Jess had tossed him over for his brother. Deciding to dismiss Landon for moment, he directed his attention solely on Jess.

Jon's hands rose in confusion. "Jess…what the hell are you doing?! This is my brother! How could you sleep with my brother?!"

Jon's wide-eyed gaze swung back to a puzzled Landon, who was wondering how any of this was his business. Jess was a grown woman and had every right to sleep with whomever she chose. Was this Jon being an overbearing ass again? But before he could ask, Jess spoke up.

"Jon, why are you here? In my house?!" Indignant, she stood ramrod straight with her hands folded on her full hips. She didn't even bother to cover up. Even if he hadn't already been treated to all of her goodies, she had nothing to hide.

Having no legitimacy for his presence, Jon quickly batted aside her question. "Right now that's not important. I have a better question." He pointed at his brother. "Were you sleeping with him when you were in my bed?"

Jon had Landon's full attention with this inquiry. All of *his* queries died on his lips the moment Jon mentioned Jess and his bed in the same sentence. With narrowing eyes, he waited for the answer.

Relaxing her stance, Jess only sighed with not wanting or feeling the need to explain herself to anyone, especially a former lover.

"Damn it Jess, answer the question!" Jon was furious. She was more concerned about him being in her home, instead of being caught with her dress up screwing his brother.

Jess rolled her eyes and sighed again. "Look Jon; our time together was nice but it's over. We both knew it would come to an end, so what is your problem? We talked about this! I thought we had this all straightened out!" Jess gestured wildly, reclaiming her indignation. She couldn't believe he was acting this way.

"What happened to no hard feelings and no strings attached, huh? We had a good time but it's over Jon!"

Resigning, Jess plopped down and back onto her bed, hoping Jon would take the hint and finally leave. The gesture was lost on him. He just couldn't let it go.

He angrily pointed back at Landon. "But that's my brother you decided to hook up with…you—"

Having heard enough, Landon halted Jon's next words with those of his own. "Wait a minute, wait a damn minute!"

Landon couldn't believe what he was hearing. He had taken the time to dispose of the condom he was wearing, in a nearby trash basket and had pulled up his briefs and pants, all while absorbing the conversation volleying back and forth between the two. He was in the process of reattaching his gun belt when it finally registered what was actually being said. Jess and Jon slept together.

Now fully aware and wanting clarification, it was his turn to confront Jess. "You were sleeping with my brother?" Landon returned Jon's earlier gesture by pointing at him.

Sitting up, Jess looked at the brothers and rolled her eyes. *These two can't be this tight assed.* Finally, she answered him, "Yes Landon, I've been with your brother. In fact, I left his bed for yours."

Out of the corner of her eye, she caught Jon's unmistakably notable flinch. This brought her a small amount of amusement. *Yes, Jon, you thought you were the shit. Now you know your brother is better. That's what you get for barreling your ass up in my house uninvited.* Jess was pretty pleased with herself.

To the brothers, "But hey, look. We're all adults here. If you two can get over yourselves for a moment, we can all have a great time together. What do you say?" With this, she smiled; pushing her still naked breasts forward as an incentive. Her fantasy of having the two brothers at once was doable if they could put aside their moral indignation.

Jon didn't even consider answering her. He briefly glanced in his brother's direction, before turning on his heels and heading for the door. He was done here. Jess had managed to turn his ego to mush, with the unwitting help of his brother. He couldn't leave there fast enough. And after Jess's parting shot, he stepped up the pace.

"Ahhh, what a shame. We could have had a great time. Landon could have shown you a few things!" she threw at him, just before he slammed her front door, leaving the windows rattling with the force.

Landon, having retrieved his senses as well, was fully dressed when Jess returned her attention to him. He was shaking his head with disgust. To think he thought she was too good for him, when in reality he was too good for her. Jess turned out to be much worse than anything that his brother could have come up with. Jon may have been a whorish pig, but even he had boundaries he wouldn't cross. Jess Ashford was despicable.

Like his brother, he had no more words for her. Even if he had more to say, he didn't see the point. The woman didn't think she had done anything wrong. He saw her with new eyes, and the image he had engraved into his memory was terrible. In his mind, Metro City's top prosecutor was the whore of whores and he was disgusted.

Landon gave the room a final sweep, making damn sure he hadn't left a single item behind. He didn't want to have to return to this woman's lair again for anything. And if fate was good to him, he would never lay eyes on her again.

Following his brother's example, he left Jess's in a hurry.

Chapter 20

Jon sat in his office despondent. He didn't know why he bothered to come in to work, because he couldn't concentrate on anything other than finding his brother banging Jess Ashford. He still couldn't believe she dumped him for Landon. Out of all the men he could have found her with it had to be his brother. No matter how hard he tried not to, his mind replayed the scene repeatedly. He remembered each moment of that night vividly. Landon screwing Jess. Landon inside Jess. Jess dumping him for Landon.

Jon rested his forehead in the palms of his hands. His ego had taken a major beating courtesy of his little brother. As brothers, they never shared much and certainly not a woman. It wouldn't have been so bad had Jess not known they were related. And it helped little that Landon was unaware of his involvement.

But did he really not know I was seeing Jess?

He immediately shook his head dismissing the thought. Landon would never do something like that. They may have had their differences, but he would never disrespect him under any circumstances. Besides, the complete and utter look of dismay on Landon's face was genuine. If it was possible, he may have been more shocked than he was. Jon sighed. If he were honest with himself, it was his own fault. When Landon first started asking about Jess, he should have told him of their involvement then.

And as if on cue, Landon tapped on his door before opening it and stepping inside. The two brothers stared at each other uncomfortably for a long moment before either of them spoke.

Swiping a hand down his face, Landon dropped into one of the two chairs near Jon's desk. Now that he was there, he didn't know what to say. And from the unease that had settled on Jon's face, neither did he. Finally, he said the only thing he could.

"Jon, you have to believe me. I didn't know." He was still wrestling with the notion that Jess was that kind of woman who would sleep with two brothers. He wondered what or who else had she done while they were seeing each other. He couldn't grasp the fact he was foolish enough to believe he was the only one.

Jon nodded his head in the affirmative before pushing out a ragged breath. "I don't blame you for any of this." He fully blamed Jess. What kind of woman was she really? Even with his reputation, there were gray areas that he strayed away from. He never thought she, especially being a woman, would stoop so low. He found he didn't know her at all. But there was something he did want to know.

"How long? I mean, when did you two…?" He let the question drift without completing it. Landon knew what he was asking.

Landon placed his hands behind his bowed head. He felt the beginnings of a tension headache brewing. "The night Trudy was killed. We met at the crime scene where she asked me to stop by her office later. From there we went back to her place." He sat up and shrugged. He should have known she was too easy. But at the time he hadn't cared.

"Look man, I didn't think you two were getting it on. The way you acted towards each other…I didn't think you even liked one another. I never would have…" He shrugged again.

Jon considered his brother. "No, this is my fault. After Lara, I decided to keep my relationships quiet. But that wasn't the reason why I didn't tell you about my involvement with Jess. I'm ashamed to admit it, but I didn't tell you because I saw it as a comeuppance. I had the woman you wanted."

Jon gave his brother a half smile before continuing. "After what happened last night, I realized I've been competing with you in my head all along. I've been hard on you because I felt the need to always 'show you how it's done', as if you are incapable of living your life without my help. It was selfish and just wrong. But believe me Landon, it stops here, right now, today." Jon tapped his desktop with his forefinger to get his point across.

By keeping him out of the loop, Jon realized he had been punishing Landon for becoming a police officer; he was jealous. Landon always lived his life according to Landon. He didn't need or want anyone's permission to be himself. Landon was free spirited where he was straight by the book and he envied him for that. But as of that moment that would all change. He owed his brother much more than an apology for what happened with Jess. He just didn't know how long it would take him to get past the incident for him to start building a real relationship with his younger brother.

Landon sat quietly while Jon talked. He had his own guilt to bear. He too had been competing, but unlike Jon he was fully aware of his transgressions. Jon had been hard on him, this much was true. But in his act of rebellion, Landon went out of his way to prove he was capable of handling his own life—in spite of what Jon thought. Whenever Jon said to go left he would take right. It hadn't mattered if what he was telling him was for his own good or not. He just automatically took the opposite route of whatever advice— or in Jon's case, bullying—was given.

Although he didn't mention any of this to his brother, he knew he had his own act to clean up. He just hoped Jon meant what he said about making amends, because he was going to continue to live his life the way he saw fit. He was a grown man capable of making all decision without his brother's input. But at the same time, he wouldn't be so bull-headed about it. He would just let Jon know when to back off.

The brothers visited a while longer, before Landon left; leaving each a little less burdened and with renewed vows to build a better brotherly relationship.

Chapter 21

Lara caught a glimpse of the shadow of someone standing just outside her dining room window. She knew who it was and she grinned. She knew it! Jon Payne wanted her. She just had to play hard to get or uninterested to get his attention. Now that he thought she no longer wanted him, he wanted her.

She had been fully aware of the late model blue sedan that had been following her for days, since she told Jon she was leaving town. He thought he could fool her by trading cars, but she knew it was him. He just couldn't stay away. However, now that he wanted *her*, she no longer wanted *him*. Jon had become boring now that he was in pursuit of her. She would punish him for causing her to lose control though. That shouldn't have ever happened. No man was allowed to treat her the way he had and get away with it. It was time for him to pay.

James pressed himself along the dully tinted stucco wall outside of Lara's house. He knew she was inside and could easily discover him, *if* he wanted her to. He had plans for her, but not now—but soon.

He had been prowling around Lara's home for days, trying to determine the right time to reveal himself and take his revenge. But when he did, he needed time to punish the bitch for leaving him. He wanted to take his time to teach her a lesson she would never forget. Unfortunately, his plans would have to wait a little while longer, due to his current case. Nevertheless, in a couple of days he would have all the time he needed to make Lara Guyton sorry she ever walked out on him.

He had already hinted for some time off at work; Matthias was more than happy to grant him the leave. He still had concerns for his workload and thought it was an excellent idea for a break. Since no one would be looking for Lara, after resigning her position at Metro Regional, no one would be the wiser to what was taking place inside her home.

Soon he would have his revenge, and once he was finished with Lara Guyton he would turn his attention back to the lady prosecutor. She needed to feel his wrath also. No woman had a right to leave him unless given permission to do so. James felt the two women needed a lesson in respect.

While he concentrated on his plot to take down his enemies, his plans ended with a sudden needle prick to the neck.

James' left eye slowly opened to a blinding light directed at his face. He had been awakened by something steadily tapping against his right temple. The pain inside his head was pounding too strongly to reason why he couldn't open his right eye. He tried moving his hand to touch it, but couldn't. He couldn't feel his arms. Had something happened to him? Had he been in an accident? How did he lose control over his arms? It took him several cloudy minutes to realize he was bound. He tried opening his mouth but found it too was restrained. Despite the growing pain in his head, he tried focusing on why he couldn't speak. Running his tongue along the minute slit between his lips revealed something was covering it.

Is that tape covering my mouth? His question was soon confirmed when he tried opening it again and found that he was gagged as well as bound.

Moving his concentration from his inability to speak, he felt something trickling down the side of his face, and from the metallic odor he feared it was blood—his blood. He tried desperately to recall what happened to him but couldn't. His head was pounding too much, not leaving room for coherent thoughts.

Catching movement at the corner of his good eye, James slowly turned his head in that direction, trying not to aggravate the already excruciating pain in his head. Focusing on the person standing near him, James's eye suddenly widened when he remembered where he was. But the memory was short lived. A single stabbing prick of pain seized him, rendering him unconscious—again.

Lara grinned at her unconscious captive. After administering a sedative, she took her fist and hit him again on the already swollen side of his face; widening the cut she had given him earlier during the first blows. She wanted him conscious but not now. She hadn't prepared her method of revenge. It wouldn't hurt for him to be out awhile longer. But when she did allow him to be awake, he would wish he wasn't.

Chapter 22

Landon Payne stared at Anderson Stone, Trudy's attorney, while he read the terms of her will. Each paragraph of the legal document elevated him to a new level of astonishment. Trudy Franklin had left him a sizable chunk of her possessions.

After a few more seconds of reading, Landon held up his hand. "Wait, wait, wait...hold up!" He had to stop him. He couldn't believe what he was hearing. "Say that again slowly, because I don't think I heard you correctly." He just knew he was dreaming.

"You heard correctly. You are the new owner of Trudy's diners," Anderson repeated.

"Did you just say *diners* as in multiples?" he asked in disbelief. With Anderson nodding, he now believed he was hearing *and* seeing things. There was no way he just nodded in the affirmative.

"So, you're saying that not only do I own *Randy's Place* or *Places*, but they were Trudy's to give?" He couldn't wrap his mind around it. Trudy owned *Randy's*

Place, plus another diner of the same name in another state. His mind hurt.

He arrived at Anderson's office a few minutes early, having no idea why he had been summoned in the first place. When he received the registered letter indicating a will, he thought someone had made a mistake. Who did he know could have actually put him in their will? The letter didn't give much detail, just requested his presence on a specified date and time. He didn't think much of it. He gathered it was all some sort of mistake that would be quickly rectified once he met with the attorney.

Anderson knew Landon was in shock not just because he was now the owner of a small chain of popular restaurants, but because he had no idea Trudy even owned the diner he was familiar with.

Anderson nodded again. "Trudy Franklin owned *Randy's* lock, stock and barrel. There are no loans or liens. She ran the restaurants debt-free. *And,*" he added, "she was in the process of opening a third store when she passed, which you will have to decide to undertake or not. She purchased the land where the restaurant would reside, but not much else. It will be up to you to do with that land from this point on."

Landon slowly shook his head, still not wanting to believe. "How is it possible that I didn't know any of this? I've been in that place hundreds of times, since I was a kid, and she never let on that she owned the place." He stopped his head shaking to scratch at the stiff stubble growing on his face. He'd been so preoccupied with discovering Jess had slept with his brother that he hadn't thought about shaving.

Anderson shrugged. "It wasn't that Trudy was keeping her ownership a secret; it was just that no one bothered to ask her. Everyone assumed, the unseen Randy was the owner. What most didn't know, Randy Franklin was Trudy's late husband, whose death had enabled her to purchase the vacant diner, abandoned by the previous owner's decades ago. She took the place and made it into what you see today."

"After Randy's death, Trudy pulled up stakes from their Southern Mississippi home and moved here for a fresh start. When she settled in Metro City, she found a place and made plans. Trudy and her husband had talked about owning a restaurant someday. Both were excellent cooks, with Randy taking his culinary skills to the level of chef, before he was killed in a boating accident. The previous owners left the restaurant fully equipped which helped cut out most of her overhead. The former owners had tried their hand at making the restaurant business work, but were unsuccessful, making their misfortune Trudy's destiny. And when it came to a name, there wasn't any other name she could have given the eatery. The diner was her and Randy's dream," Anderson explained.

And the second restaurant?" Landon asked.

"The second restaurant in Arkansas came about by accident. She was there visiting a friend when she ran across a historic building that had been vacant for years. The rustic charm of the place drew her, so she decided to open a second location. Trudy was an excellent judge of character and was savvy enough to hire trusted personnel to run the place. She was so pleased with the outcome of that location that she made plans to open a third."

"What the hell am I going to do with one restaurant let along two?" Landon was beyond perplexed. With his ever changing work schedule; there was no way he had the time to devote to running either diner. Not to mention he didn't know the first thing about running a business.

"The way Trudy has things set up, the diners practically run themselves. The cooks and wait staff she employed know the businesses inside out and are a loyal bunch. They will do whatever they can to help you. It would be a shame if either *Randy's* was shut down. The one here is an icon in this city and is quickly becoming so in Arkansas." Anderson understood Landon's dilemma and sympathized with him, but Trudy wanted the restaurants to remain open no matter what.

"Look, if you need more help, I have a friend in the management industry, who would be more than happy to help you out. Trudy had a great head for business and hadn't a need for management beyond consulting with this company from time to time when she wanted to make some improvements."

Anderson pulled a business card from his top desk drawer and handed it to him. "This management group can give you everything you need to help you run things smoothly."

Landon took the card and read the name, "*Tenney, Faulkner & Lowe – Property Management, LLC.*" He sighed. If one of his options was to keep the diners open, he'd better seek help.

Chapter 23

Detective Eric Valero's eyes widened when multiple photos of the new prosecutor came tumbling from the down turned manila envelope onto his desk. There were dozens of them. All of the lady D.A. in various sexual positions with various men. As he casually sifted through the pile, he whistled when he came across one of her with Metro City's former gangbanging mayor, Craven Wallace. It seemed the former mayor's banging wasn't just confined to crime alone, unless Jess Ashford was somehow a part of the mayor's criminal schemes. For her sake he sure hoped not. But either way, if any of those photos should ever see the light of day, she could probably kiss her job as prosecutor goodbye, at least in that city. Metro City's citizens were fed up with the constant barrage of negative publicity that had descended unapologetically on their city.

Sorting through the rest of the images, he came across the photos of men he knew and respected. Eric frowned. "What is this woman into?"

The deeper he dug through the pile the more faces he recognized. He retrieved a lockbox from a locked desk draw and placed three photos inside before relocking both securely. He would hold on to those until, if and when, they were ever needed to be shared. Neither of the men deserved to have their personal lives dragged through the mud. As far as he was concerned, they lived exemplary lives and should continue to do so. He briefly considered setting a few more aside, but thought better of it. He was certain that whoever sent them was very familiar with its contents. On the off chance the photos were reveal, the sender might take offense if too many were held back. Two photos missing from the collection could easily be seen as an over-sight, more than that could create a problem.

Picking the envelope up again, but this time by a corner in case there were fingerprints, he examined it for a return address to indicate where the photos had come from, but there wasn't one. The only indication of the sender was the post mark that meant the packet was mailed in Metro City, which didn't mean much. The sender could still be someone from out of town; out of the country even. It would be easy to pay someone to drop the envelope in a local mailbox. And if there were any legible prints at all, he would guess they probably belonged to some local vagrant given a few dollars for the task. Whoever sent them was careful and on a particular mission. And with only one common denominator in each of the photos, it wasn't hard to deduce who the target was. If he had to guess, the men in the photos were just collateral damage. It appeared Jess Ashford had gotten someone's back up and now it was time for payback.

Eric sighed. Could the day get any worse? On top of everything else that was happening, someone had to choose this moment to add the photos to the chaos. James Harrison, one of Matthias Bennett's attorneys, was missing and he didn't have a lead as to where he could have disappeared to. There was no clue from his cell phone, for it was either destroyed or turned off. He hadn't made any purchases or withdrawn any money in over three days.

Matthias had been unconcerned by his absence until James missed an important court date. According to Matthias, for James Harrison to miss anything that had to do with the law, and especially any court proceedings, sent off warning bells all over the place. It seemed that Mr. Harrison loved his job to a point of almost obsession.

Forgetting the photos for a moment, Eric picked up a file containing cases James was working on. Browsing through the pages in the folder, there didn't seem to be any threats among the people listed there. Most of the cases involved, hadn't gone to trial yet, so there couldn't be any angry clients looking for revenge because of dissatisfaction in the courtroom.

Eric sighed. He would have to do an extensive background search on the man to see what enemies popped up from that angle. For him to disappear the way he had, there was more than likely foul play involved. He just hoped when they did find him it wouldn't be too late.

Needing to get the ball rolling, Eric reached for his desk phone when there was a knock at his door. Remembering the photos, he quickly swept the pile into an open desk draw; closing it, before inviting his visitor inside. There was no need for anyone to see them unless it was necessary. And at the moment, Jess Ashford had done no wrong.

Eric grinned when his now fiancé, KT, entered the room with a colleague, Kobe West. He moved around his desk to give her a proper greeting. Ignoring Kobe for the moment, he pulled KT into his arms for a long lingering kiss.

Eric had proposed to KT three nights ago, in one of the city's upscale restaurants. After he placed the emerald cut, four carat diamond ring on her finger, she agreed to marry him without hesitation. He was the happiest man alive.

Kobe cleared his throat, "Get a room." He smiled when Eric released KT to embrace him. "I see the newness of being engaged hasn't worn off for you two."

"Man, not on your life. If you think I'm happy now, just wait until I get this woman in front of a minister." Eric clapped him on the back.

"I feel the same way," KT chimed in. She couldn't have been any happier if she tried. Who would have thought a chance meeting at a crime scene would have netted her a husband?

KT Ellis had been working as a bodyguard for Justin Graham, one of Metro City's prominent entrepreneurs, when someone shot at him at his home. She and Eric met when he was dispatched to Justin's house after the incident.

"Kobe, I guess I don't have to ask why you're here." He checked his watch before turning to KT, hoping he hadn't forgotten something. "Babe, do we have an appointment I forgot about? He was surprised to see the two together considering they both worked from different agencies.

KT kissed his cheek. "Nope, I'm here on business. I'm between assignments at the moment, so Kobe asked if I would help find James."

"And since you're working on the case, we came to compare notes and see if there is anything that either of us has missed," Kobe added.

Returning to his desk, Eric picked up the folder again. "Well from my end, there isn't much to go on. All I have is useless information at the moment." He let the folder fall back onto his desk. He hoped they had more than he had.

Retrieving a folder of his own, Kobe handed Eric the contents. "Well, as you can see, we have a bit more. A part from his stellar record as a litigator, the man has a rather shady personal life. I've traced him back to several sex clubs located in California. I don't know how this may fit in with his disappearance, if at all. But it could be that a jilted lover decided to take out revenge for something involving a relationship or activity at one of these clubs." Kobe produced the list of clubs and handed it to Eric.

Eric scratched at his chin. The mention of sex brought him back to Jess Ashford. Although he only gave the photos a cursory assessment, is it possible James

Harrison is among the host of photos in his drawer? Knowing he could trust the two, he pulled the drawer open to retrieve the stack of raunchy pictures. They collectively hit his desk with a *splat*.

"See if you can find him in any of these," he told Kobe. Eric rubbed at his eyes. He didn't want to look at them anymore today if he didn't have to.

Kobe and KT both sorted through the stack.

"Are you kidding me? Jess Ashford?" KT asked as she picked up photo after photo, each more eye opening than the last.

Eric nodded. "There is one particularly enthralling one in there that I think you will find quite interesting." He nodded at the scattered photos.

"You mean this one?" Kobe held the one with Jess performing a lewd sex act on their former mayor." Eric nodded again.

"O-m-g!" KT handed the photo she was holding to Kobe. Even though the couple was engaged in a sex act in the foreground, she spotted the man instantly.

Recognizing the man as well, Kobe's jaw clenched before handing it off to Eric. "Did you catch the person standing in the shadows on this one?" Kobe asked him.

Eric's brow furrowed. "Where?" Kobe pointed to the lean, shirtless figure standing in the back of the room. "What the hell…is that Romaro Grey? How the hell did I miss *him*!"

Kobe's mouth tightened again. He braced himself for that old familiar pang of guilt and anger to sweep over him, but there was none. He quietly sighed in relief. He'd finally forgiven himself for Bria's death at the hands of Romaro Grey. He had time and Blake Steele to thank for that.

"Here he is!" KT had returned to the stack and found a photo that contained both Jess Ashford *and* James Harrison.

Eric frowned. Now Jess Ashford was officially involved in his investigation and he would have to question her today. But he preferred to do it without the help of his fiancé. The two women had not hit it off on their first introduction. And now that KT had seen the photos, although he knew she would remain professional, he also knew she wouldn't miss an opportunity to let the woman know she was aware of her dirty little secret.

He should have listened to her when she told him something wasn't quite right with Ms. Ashford. And if she had anything to do with James Harrison's disappearance, soon the whole world would know what she's been hiding.

As if reading Eric's mind, KT continued sorting through the photos, but with a smug smile of satisfaction.

Chapter 24

A constant, mind irritating sound pulled James from an unconscious state for a second time. Awake but drowsy, he tried focusing on the source of the maddening noise. With his one good eye, he blinked several times to clear away the fuzziness. He was confused, but he finally realized the noise was someone singing. Why would someone be singing and where could he be to hear such an ear grating tone.

He recoiled as the awful singing drew closer. The noise, coupled with the dizziness from the drugs, and the wound on the side of his head, made it almost impossible to put together a rational thought. The person who was emitting the unwelcomed clamor was now right in front of him. Summoning all of his strength, James lifted his head and focused. It was Lara. She was the one singing.

Remembering the tape, James was relieved to find it gone. With applied effort, he ran the tip of his tongue over dry cracked lips, before opening his mouth to speak. The sound that came forth was rough, but audible.

"Lara…Lara what's going on? Where am I?"

Lara's grin was wide. "You're in my house, silly. Don't you remember Jon?"

It was a rhetorical question, because she knew full well that he couldn't remember most of what happened to him, only recalling bits and pieces of his ordeal. She had injected enough Versed into his system to make sure he didn't. She'd given him his fourth dose just that morning. Dr. Guyton had taken great care with that one. The one before had him out for so long she thought he would never come around. And just to make sure he could awaken at her command, she had thumped him on the side of his head only to give him another injection after he came to. But now, it was time they talked.

Lara had discontinued her medication some time ago, so she didn't realize that it wasn't Jon Payne bound in her dining room, but her ex, James Harrison. Her psychotic mind had easily morphed James into Jon. Dr. Lara Guyton's sane mind had completely vacated the premises.

Lara waited until 'Jon' positioned himself at her patio door. She knew he thought she was inside the house oblivious to his presence. She had prepared for his return all week. When she was sure he was distracted, she quietly exited the front door and slipped around back, behind him; injecting him with a strong sedative. She was grateful he chose to stalk her near the sliding glass patio doors. His position made light work of her dragging him inside quickly and quietly. Even with the privacy fence, you never knew who could be watching.

Pulling him up onto one of the dining room chairs had been a struggle, but she hardly noticed. Lara Guyton's mind was occupied with extracting her revenge. Once he was seated and bound, she placed Duct tape over his mouth. She couldn't have the neighbors calling the police because of all the screaming that was sure to come. What she had planned for the good doctor, she wanted time to administer without being interrupted. Once her prey was immobilized she searched his pockets for his car keys. After finding the blue sedan parked up the block, she drove it into the unoccupied space in her double vehicle garage. She could take her time with him and no one would be the wiser.

Lara blinked at a muddled James. Needing him to focus, she snapped her fingers before his face to gather his attention. "Come on Jon, stay with me."

Confused, James's brow furrowed. "Jon? Why do you keep calling me Jon? That's not my name and you damn well know it!" James had gathered his wits and was livid that this crazy bitch held him captive.

Uncertainty began to prick Lara's mind with James's claim that he was not Jon. While her former rational self, fought to be heard, her maniacal smile slipped for just a moment; giving way to a barrage of back and forth images that was akin to a static plagued television picture that faded in and out of frequency. James Harrison's face briefly broke through the fuzziness, only to give way to Jon Payne's permanent return. Regaining her composure, Lara's full smile returned with him.

"Jon Payne, don't you try to trick me," she admonished. "I would know you anywhere, baby." With her mania firmly in place, she stared unblinkingly at a baffled James.

This bitch has slipped into the deep end.

James increasingly realized he was in real trouble. Strapped to a chair, he had a crazy recollection of a movie he once saw, where some unhinged lunatic held a man captive in her house; torturing him just for the hell of it. Lara fit the character perfectly. Dr. Lara Guyton had gone full Annie Wilkes on his ass, beatings and all. He liked Stephen King's stories, but not enough to find himself living one.

But even with this new revelation, James became agitated. "Listen Lara, I'm not Jon! I'm your man James, see? James Harrison. Look at me!" He had to get her to see he wasn't Jon Payne. He rationalized that she would release him if she came to her senses. And if by chance she did, he was going to beat the crap out of her crazy ass.

Unmoved, Lara continued her singing; completely drowning out his pleas. Her grin held its place, while she tore off a fresh piece of Duct tape, placing it firmly over 'Jon's' mouth. It was time to teach him a lesson on how to treat women; mainly on how to treat her.

Finished with that task, she laid the roll of tape on the dining table to admire her handy work. Not quite satisfied with the single piece of silvery gray strip, she retrieved the roll and applied layer after layer, by completely winding the tape about his mouth and around his head several times before she was satisfied.

James's heart beat wildly in terror, as Lara discarded the finished roll and left the room. He had to do something. He had to get out of there. The woman was out of her mind and capable of anything. He tried rocking the chair from side to side; testing the strength of his bindings. But she had used that same roll of tape to bind his arms and legs to the chair; leaving little room for movement. With his good eye, he frantically searched around the room for any help. His head snapped at attention when Lara returned from the kitchen with one hand hidden behind her back.

"Jonny, I have a surprise for you," she sing-sang.

James's eye widened in stark horror when Lara produced her surprise from its hiding place—a very large and very sharp carving knife. He tried in vain to free himself from his restraints, as she closed the gap between them. With her free hand, she gleefully unbuttoned his shirt. Then using the sharp point of the blade, cut away the undershirt beneath it; nicking him several times in the process.

Ignoring James's terrified one-eyed gaze and muffled screams, Dr. Lara Guyton proceeded to carve her full name into 'Jon Payne's' rapidly heaving chest.

Chapter 25

Oh my god, some one knows my secret!

Jess Ashford listened in horror while Detective Eric Valero described the contents of the packet he'd received earlier that day.

Jess had been all smiles when Eric arrived at her office that afternoon. After the Payne brothers bailed on her, she placed him back on her list of pending bed partners. She'd heard the office gossip that the handsome detective had gotten himself engaged to that KT person. It didn't matter. She still planned to have him. Where there was a will there was always a way around jealous girlfriends.

While Eric was making small talk, Jess was scheming on how to persuade him to have one last prenuptial fling. And if he agreed, anything could happen. Once he got a taste of her, he may even forget he asked the stuck up bitch to marry him. She was known to break the strongest of wills and she had no doubt that Eric Valero would be no different. But that was all before he ended the pleasantries and stated his purpose for the visit.

James Harrison was missing. She didn't know how
or why and didn't particularly care. And she especially
didn't understand why Eric's investigation brought him to
her doorstep. She didn't see how anything remotely
concerning James' life had to do with her. Although,
heaven forbid, his investigation took a turn criminally, then
she would be more than ready to sit up and take notice to
bring the culprit to justice. Otherwise, James's
disappearance wasn't her problem and she told the
detective as much. At that point, she didn't see how she
could be of any help to him.

But her tone soon changed once he started
questioning if she had a *personal* connection to James; one
she vehemently denied. She didn't know where the
detective was going with his line of questioning, but she
didn't have long to wait to find out.

After her flat denial of not knowing James outside
of a courtroom, Eric revealed that he had undeniable proof
that he knew differently. Thinking he was bluffing, Jess
stood her ground. It sounded as if he was on a fact finding
exhibition; that was until he produced the damning photo of
her and James in a very real and very vivid sexual
copulation.

Jess was speechless. Her mind ran in all sorts of directions at once. She nearly fainted when a copy of the photo landed on the desk before her. District attorney or not, Jess Ashford just became more than a person of interest in James Harrison's disappearance. She was now Eric's only suspect.

After a moment of allowing the existence of the photo to settle in, he informed her it wasn't the only one. There were many more of its kind. Jess wanted to throw up. According to Eric, there were dozens of photos depicting her in various compromising positions with various men. And according to some of the time stamps, some of the images spanned over several years. He explained to her that most of the photos appeared to be still shots snipped from videos. He also informed her that the sender of the packet was unknown.

That meant photos *and* videos of her personal life were floating around just waiting to expose her. And there was no way of stopping it. Who could have done this? She had never consented to any photos let alone videos. It never crossed her mind that some of her connections could be filming their encounters. Why should she. Those men had just as much to lose as she did. Who could want to hurt her like this? Who would risk their own hide just to skin hers?

And the photo with her and James was taken in her office. That meant someone had set up a hidden camera in her private office and possibly her home! Her mind raced with all the horrid possibilities; desperately searching for a culprit.

Coming up empty, Jess soon realized it didn't matter who or why. She was finished. Even if by some miracle the other photos the detective had in his possession never saw the light of day, the person who sent them had all the fire power to destroy her at will, at any given moment. And from the way the damning things were presented, the person who possessed them would no doubt do just that.

Swallowing the hard lump that had formed in her throat, Jess finally found her voice. "Detective…" She had to clear her throat before continuing. "Detective, I assure you that I had nothing to do with James's disappearance. We stopped seeing each other weeks ago. Yes we had a sexual relationship, but it was brief and was really over before it had a chance to gain momentum." Jess closed her eyes. She couldn't believe this was happening to her.

Eric noticed how she refused to acknowledge the existence of the photos. He nodded before asking his next question. "Did you end the relationship or did he?" His pen was poised over a notepad, waiting for her answer.

"Look, I know where this is going. I ended it and he was fine with it. We both knew going in that it was short term. People like us rarely involve ourselves in long term commitments. It takes away from the high."

Jess decided to just speak freely about her lifestyle. Eric had seen all there was to see of her. Those photos had exposed her in more ways than she cared to acknowledge. Her secret was out. There was no use in hiding anymore, at least not from him.

Eric made some notes. "When was the last time you saw James Harrison?"

Settling more comfortably in her chair, Jess relaxed and reclaimed her confidence. "The last time I saw James was in Judge Williams' courtroom nearly two weeks ago. It was a prehearing and we were in opposition over an upcoming trial. A trial that was supposed to start around the time you said he went missing. When he didn't show up for court, Judge Williams just postponed until James could be contacted for a new trial date. After that, I just shrugged it off until the new date was appointed. I didn't realize the man was missing."

The next question pulled Eric out of his element. He had zero knowledge of her preferred lifestyle; therefore, he couldn't gauge any characteristics or habits associated with the culture. But he had to ask.

"Are people in your circle known to disappear like this?" Jess knew what he was asking and shook her head in the negative.

She explained, "Those of us, who have what you may call a normal public life, wouldn't dare take a chance of their hidden life being exposed in anyway. Any kind of disappearance would send up all sorts of red flags; flags that would cause colleagues, family—anyone close, to ask questions. The least light on our lives the better. We can't take the chance of anyone beyond our realm, to discover us or we could lose everything."

It was a common fear that outsiders would find out and expose them for the societal misfits they'd been branded. Each member in her world knew there could or would be a someday, and Jess knew her time had come. Someone hated her enough to make certain of it.

Satisfied with her answers, Eric rose from his seat, before he remembered the other photo that had piqued his interest. "I have one last question for you and it has nothing to do with my investigation." Eric retrieved the photograph from his jacket pocket. It was the one with Romero Grey standing in the background.

"How do you know this man, here?" He handed her the photograph and pointed to Romero.

Jess frowned. "I was in Jamaica a few years back, vacationing with one of my friends. At the time, we thought it would be fun if we added a third to the party and asked the hotel's manager to join us. My companion had partied with him before. But in hindsight, we both wished we'd never met the man. Especially after learning he had murdered someone in the States and was running an international prostitution ring. Let's just say, he was one of my two regrettable missteps in this life." Jess handed the photo back to him.

"And the other?" Eric asked.

She gave him a half smile before she answered. "If you truly do have in your possession a chronicle of my lifestyle in photos, then I have no doubt there's a photograph of me and Craven Wallace. Everyone else seems to be there. And before you ask, Craven was just another hookup, nothing more. But you're free to investigate further, although you have to know, if I had any involvement in Craven's activities, you would have discovered it long before now."

Eric nodded.

Eric believed Jess Ashford wasn't involved in James Harrison's disappearance. The woman seemed sincere. Although he had been fooled before, he didn't think that was the case this time. One thing was for certain, he felt sorry for Jess's plight. He didn't think a person's lifestyle, inside the boundaries of the law, was anyone's business. Had she been a man, the scandal would blow over in record time. But because she was a woman, she would never live it down.

Someone wanted Jess Ashford crucified and they were taking an agonizing approach in the process. The longer it took for her secret to be exposed, the longer her enemy had power over her. It wasn't a matter of if this person would expose her, but when.

Eric sighed. The one suspect he had a lead on he crossed off his list. He hoped KT and Kobe had better luck looking deeper into the man's background, because at this point he didn't know where to turn.

Chapter 26

Kane jumped at the sound that broke the silence in the expensively decorated room. It was the buzzer from the buildings intercom system. The doorman was ringing his residence.

Swiping a nervous hand down his face, he got up to answer it. "Yes?"

"Mr. Alonso, your takeout has arrived," the doorman informed him.

Swiping at his face again, Kane vaguely comprehended he needed a shave. "Send him up Andre."

Releasing the speaker button, he fished a wad of bills from his rumpled pocket to pay the delivery boy. His face wasn't the only thing that needed tending to. Although he was bare chested, he was still wearing the jeans from two days ago.

Kane had been holed up for days in his downtown apartment since the unsuccessful gang battle; only showering and changing clothes if he thought to. He hadn't been back on the streets for fear of being recognized. He was sure the old dude at the diner had given the police a full description. The man had gotten a good eyeful and it was only a matter of time before they found him. But then again, maybe not. It seemed like months, and the police hadn't shown up on his doorstep. No one knew about his spot in the upscale high rise in what was considered the city's bougie downtown district; not even his boys knew he lived there. In fact, no one knew exactly where he lived.

After his grandmother died, he took over her rent payments and only crashed there whenever it was necessary. Usually, when he was hanging with his boys or making moves to secure their rightful territory after the bosses went to prison. Before then, he hadn't been back to his childhood home since he left as a teen. Prior to that, he crashed at his boy Ice's place when he was too tired or intoxicated to make the trek downtown without drawing the attention of the police.

But once the street wars started, he had been sneaking away more to his 'real' home; a condominium worth over a half a million dollars in the heart of downtown Metro City. He bought the place a few years back when the money was really rolling in. unlike his crew, he didn't waste his funds on stupid shit like jewelry, kicks or fancy rides, all the things that was sure to attract the wrong kind of attention. Besides, he had bigger dreams. Kane squirreled enough money away, until he had enough to buy the place out right. This was his home, his sanctuary. Nothing touched him here and most importantly none of the residents knew who he really was or what he did for a living and he planned to keep it that way. His sister wasn't the only one who changed her last name. In bougie-land he was known as Alonso Carpenter, entrepreneur. No one knew what his business entailed and never asked. As long as he had the full purchase amount for the condo, they didn't much care.

Kane thought about his sister Shelby. He often thought about her and felt guilty for leaving her behind. After the trash—that was their parents—abandoned them, he got to the point where he didn't want to be around any reminders of them. His grandmother use to have all kinds of photos of her son, their father, around the house. There were photos of him as a boy in elementary school, high school and the one with him sporting his college graduation swag with honor cords and all.

Elsa Kane was most proud of the one taken at his father's college graduation ceremony. Her only child had grown up and made her proud, by becoming a college graduate; an achievement that she didn't get to share, because she wasn't invited to celebrate that proud day.

Even still, her son could do no wrong. After their mother left and he dumped him and Shelby on her, Elsa Kane still held her son in the highest esteem.

But all that changed the day he took each and every photo he could find in the house and burned them to a blackened pile of ash. Kane hated his parents, but he hated his father most. After their mother Tina left, his father became the only anchor he had to hold onto. But instead of becoming the father he and Shelby needed, he tossed them aside in favor of himself. Kane was grateful his sister was too young to remember their parents. She was better off not knowing them and he told her so when she had gotten old enough to ask about them.

But he should have been there for her, even after he left their grandmother's place. For this, he was sorry. Years later he realized he had done the exact same thing to her as their parents had, and for that he was repentant and greatly ashamed. The night Trudy Franklin was killed he vowed to make things right with his sister. He realized life was too short and he needed to make amends for his own wrong doings.

Kane knew exactly where she was and had been keeping tabs on her since she escaped the neighborhood and graduated from college. He had a friend at her bank who gave him her account number in which he used to frequently deposit money into her savings account. He knew she knew the money was from him. But he didn't know if she understood this was his way of asking for her forgiveness. He hoped so. When he discovered she'd legally changed her last name he didn't blame her. In fact, he applauded her. He knew it was her way of finally accepting that they really had no parents. Her keeping the last name meant she was still holding out hope to find them or them finding her. He was proud of his little sister. She had managed to do everything right and make a legitimate name for herself; unlike him, hiding out from the police even if his surroundings were safe and comfortable.

Although he did feel safe there, he had been contemplating purchasing a unit in a new building developed by Bennett Co., a local construction broker. Any purchase snagged in Bennett Towers was considered the buy of the century, whether it was residential or retail. His place was great, but Bennett Towers was considered supreme. With the amenities it boasted, he wouldn't have to leave the building for anything. And with the fatal outcome of the 'little scrimmage' the other night, the idea of moving became more and more enticing.

Kane was beginning to feel it was time to make some other changes too; like leave the gang life. He had accomplished what he set out to do, and that was to make money. And according to his investment portfolio, he had done just that. He had accumulated enough money to carry over into a couple of lifetimes. So there was no real reason to keep risking his life. For what? City blocks that were owned by no one but the city itself? And if the new D.A. had her way, all of their playhouses were about to come crashing down anyway.

Yes, it was time for him to get out of the game. For one thing it was senseless and for another, he couldn't watch another person die. It really bothered him that old lady at the diner had gotten caught up in his mess. He shouldn't have ever gone in there. He should have just kept running until he found another place to hide. And now, because of his actions, someone was dead. And if he had any kind of luck, his crew thought he was dead too. It would make it easier to transition into his newly planned legitimate life. He had avoided all contact with any of them since that night. He had had enough of the streets.

When his doorbell sounded, Kane moved to answer it. With the total amount for his food in hand, plus a healthy tip, he opened the door to his favorite delivery boy. But what he found was a bullet to the head instead.

Chapter 27

Detective Eric Valero raked long tapered fingers through his thick, nearly black mass of hair. The street life had crossed the tracks—so to speak—and had brought the fight uptown, leaving the wealthy residents outraged, and rightly so. They paid good money to be protected from just this sort of element. But somehow, it found its way through the eloquent foyer and rode the elevator up to the victim's tastefully decorated apartment.

Well, he didn't have to worry about the last suspect connected to Trudy's murder. He was lying face down with a bullet hole to the forehead that exited through the back of his skull. According to the body's position, he assumed the perpetrator rolled him over after searching his turned out front pockets, to retrieve his wallet. Surprisingly, the high grade leather holder was still lying beside him.

Squatting, Eric retrieved a pen from his pocket to sort through it. As far as he could see there was nothing taken. There was a couple of hundreds inside, along with a few credit cards, all platinum, in the name of Alonso Carpenter. No wonder they couldn't find Kane. He vaguely wondered what other names the former gangster had used.

He stood to further survey the crime scene. What was this all about? But the bigger question was who did it? Trudy's two actual killers were locked up in jail awaiting trial. Was the hit made by their fellow bangers for revenge or was this something else entirely? He hoped it was the former, because if it wasn't, they had a new problem on their hands. But if it was a revenge hit, why search his pockets with nothing taken? Or was there something taken?

Eric had many questions. Like, how could Alonso Kane afford a place like this and why didn't the police know it existed? Was crime paying that well on the streets of Metro City? He had to assume Kane took great pains in keeping this place a secret, because up until this point, the building's tenants didn't know they had a violent criminal living among them. Eric concluded that it wasn't secret enough, because someone found him and killed him.

"Detective?" One of Eric's officers grabbed his attention.

"Yes?"

"It's been reported that a house the victim is connected to, is fully engulfed in fire. The fire chief says they won't know until after they do their investigation as to whether or not its arson, but he suspects that it is."

"Who does the house belong to?" Eric asked.

The officer flipped through his notebook. "One of the banks here in town owns the house, but it's been rented out for years to an Elsa Kane, the decedent's grandmother, who died some time ago"

"Thanks officer." Eric frowned. In his line of work, there were no such things as coincidences. Kane killed in his home and now his grandmother's place burns to the ground? This was sounding like more than just gangland payback. What the hell was really going on?

Shelby stared at her brother's lifeless body lying on the coroner's cold, stainless steel table. It had been years since she'd seen Alonso and just like she predicted, he ended up at her workplace.

As her eyes searched over his relaxed features, she thought she would feel something, anything, but nothing came. There wasn't any grief or anger. She should have been still angry with him for leaving her all those years ago. She loved her brother and was hurt when he left without looking back. Never once coming to check on her to see if she was all right. Even though she knew it was him, who added money to her bank account every other month, it wasn't what she wanted. She wanted her family; she wanted an explanation. But now she wouldn't have either.

Shelby shook her head. What a wasted life. Her brother had always been smart and knew more ways than one to make money. She couldn't understand, with a mind like his, why he didn't attend college and make something of himself and now it was too late. Alonso was the only family she had left. She was now truly all alone.

Jon stood just beyond the open double doors in the shadows watching Shelby. He'd heard from one of the nurses upstairs that the coroner had brought in one of her relatives. Kane had her name and information in a rolodex in his home office. Written in bold black ink and underlined twice were the words 'my sister'. The man lying dead on the table was her brother.

Standing there watching her, he realized he knew close to nothing about her. He worked with her every day and he didn't even know she had a brother. But to be brutally honest, he hadn't cared. He hadn't cared about any of the women he worked with; those he's slept with or not. It was always about him nothing more. After licking the wounds inflicted by Jess, he became aware of what an asshole he really was. So when he heard about Shelby, he went in search of her. To do what, he didn't know. To be there for her? Maybe, but why? He didn't know her and that was the problem.

He watched her a while longer before turning to head back upstairs. He didn't know her or her brother's situation, but he knew when someone had unresolved emotions bottled up inside, and Shelby was way over due for the pressure to be released. He vowed he would be there for her when it did.

Chapter 28

Kobe stepped into his fourth dimly lit establishment of the night. The club was much like the others, with way too much activity for his tastes. He wasn't a prude by any means, but some of the open air sexual activity he witnessed in the past few hours made him cringe. He'd heard and read about sex clubs, but up until this case, he had never had the displeasure of patronizing one. And after entering the first club, he could truly say he never wanted to step foot in another one once this case was over. People were more depraved than he imagined.

Pulling a stool up to the bar, he tried not to make eye contact with the busty redhead who was making a beeline towards him, only to be stopped by one of the other patrons, whom she quickly found interesting. He was relieved. He had never had to fight off as many women *or* men as he had since landing in this unseemly world. He had been to the west coast many times, but never had the opportunity or reason to experience the seedier side of it until now.

The bartender materialized in front of him. "What can I get you?" The bored man shouted over the pulsing music. To Kobe, he looked as if he had been working there far too long to let anything in the place surprise him. The man didn't even blink when a couple at the end of the bar decided they needed to feed their sexual desires right then and there. Indifference covered his delicate features while he waited for Kobe's answer.

"Just give me whatever you have on tap," he told him. While he waited for his beer, Kobe tried not to let on that he was there for anything other than a good time, which was becoming more impossible to do. It took everything in him not to run out of the place for a very hot cleansing shower. But he had no other choice. He learned from the first place he visited, asking questions made people bottle up, unless he went along with the vibe of the place. Fitting in meant he had to grin and bear it when a woman came on to him in order to get any information. After his first encounter, he decided to stick close to the staff for information.

When the bartender returned with is beer, he slid two bills and a photo of James Harrison towards him. The twenty was for his drink and the other for information.

"I'm looking for my brother and his girlfriend," he lied. "Our dad died and I need to locate him before the funeral." Kobe learned people were more apt to help if there was grief involved. Although, as he looked around the room, there was plenty of grief to be had right there. While a man was happily humping one woman in a corner, another one was standing nearby; presumably the man's wife or girlfriend and she didn't look too happy about the situation. She only watched a few seconds before stomping off towards the exit; the man never stopped his sexual onslaught to go after her.

The bartender picked up the photo *and* the larger bill, pocketing it quickly before placing the other in the cash register. He nodded. "Yeah James. He used to come here a lot before he hooked up with one of the other regulars. I hear the two are like married or something now." He shrugged as if to say, to each his own.

He handed the photo back to Kobe. "Man, I don't know what it was about that woman, but she sure seemed to keep him interested. James has probably screwed everyone in this place and then some. I always thought he and the girl he shacked up with were…you know like polar opposites. James liked it rough and all that came with it. The woman, even though she was somewhat a regular, always played it safe; staying away from the heavy handed players. But I guess he talked her into it for the long haul, because I haven't seen either of them in a long time. They must have found somewhere else to play."

"Do you remember the woman's name?"

The man nodded. "He called her Dr. Lara. Bragged about her being some big time surgeon, neuro… or something, which surprised me. But I guess surgeons like kinky too." The man shrugged again.

Grateful for the information, Kobe laid another hundred-dollar bill on the bar top and left. He now had something to work with and hopefully he wouldn't have to frequent another sex club as long as he lived. He was glad he talked KT out of coming with him. Eric would have had his head, had he exposed her to this dark underworld.

Chapter 29

Jon stared wide-eyed at the talking head on his flat screen television mounted on the wall of his home gym. He'd been running on his treadmill when the breaking news ticker came across the bottom of the muted screen. He hadn't really paid it any mind until Jess Ashford's smiling face appeared. He stopped the machine immediately and turned up the volume.

"At midnight this morning, gossip site *Do Tail All*, known for publicizing photos and videos of celebrities in questionable and compromising positions, posted numerous photos of Metro City's top prosecuting attorney Jess Ashford. The photos are of Ashford with various men in various sexual situations. Although the more risqué portions of the images have been blurred out, we caution that viewer discretion is advised."

The news commentator continued as photo after photo appeared on the TV screen. Faces of men Jon knew, but many more of those he didn't. Holding his breath, he waited for his image to flash across the screen, but it never came. He didn't know what to think. Was that all of them?

Or were there so many that they just didn't have time to air them all?

Workout forgotten, he leaped off the treadmill to claim a spot on the sofa. Jon desperately flipped from news channel to news channel, searching for any clue that he was among those photographed with Jess. His stomach turned over into knots when he recalled the newscaster saying something about a website.

"Oh my god!" Bolting from the gym he took the stairs two at a time to his home office. He had to check the websites. Clicking on the one that was trending, he spent several minutes scrolling through the photos posted. His image was not to be found. He wanted to feel relief, but he couldn't. It was early and there was still a chance he could show up before the day was over.

Another thought occurred to him. Not only was his photo not among Jess's sex partners, but neither was his brother's. He picked up the desk phone to call him, but changed his mind. At this point he didn't know what he should do. Leaving Landon alone for now, he turned on the TV to see what else was going on.

The twenty-four hour news channel led with a stock video of Jess leaving the courthouse, before the images turned ugly. The news reporter was saying that they had tried contacting the popular D.A. but were unsuccessful. The reporter went on to speculate what it meant for Jess Ashford and Metro City's prosecuting office. The young man predicted that Ms. Ashford's tenure as District Attorney was over, if not her career.

Jon swiped a hand down his face. He wondered if it was only a matter of time before the reporter would be speculating about him.

Landon walked into the unusually quiet precinct with a purse snatcher in handcuffs. He had settled the man into a chair to wait processing, before he noticed the strange hush that had fell over the building. The only thing he heard was the volume of several televisions.

Curious to see what was going on, he rounded the corner to the common room and came to a complete stop. Everyone in the room was glued to the flat screens mounted around the precinct's bland walls. He touched the first person he saw on the shoulder to ask what was going on.

"Man, where you been? The story of the century just hit the news. Our new lady D.A. literally just had her tail spread out all over everywhere…TV, newspaper, internet, you name it. Dude, that woman has been screwing half the country."

Remembering Landon's interest in Jess, the officer took a closer look at him. "Ain't you glad you didn't get a chance to hit that?" He turned back to the screen without awaiting Landon's answer.

Still puzzled as to what his colleague was talking about, he turned his attention to the screen nearest him.

"If you're just joining us and wonder what the uproar is about, let me update you," the news commentator was saying.

"Metro City's district prosecuting attorney, Jess Ashford, has been exposed in some very graphic sexual situations, via photos posted earlier this morning on the gossip site, *Do Tail All*. Ms. Ashford's sexual partners, range from politicians, dentists, to one of our very own police commanders, Terrance Hanlon. And Ms. Ashford didn't stop there; she was also photographed locking bodies with her personal driver Rafe Santiago in her home."

"Aw man not Rafe! His wife is going to kill him." This was from one of the onlookers.

It was bad enough to discover his brother was in bed with Jess, now Rafe? Landon had no idea his former partner was sleeping with the, oh, so popular DA. He and Rafe came out of the academy together. They were friends.

"Man, if I'd known all that action was going on, I would have taken that de-*tail*," another one of the onlookers quipped with everyone laughing; everyone except Landon. Some of the others offered their lewd comments, before everyone quieted down again to hear the rest of the news.

"But the biggest shocker came when former corrupt mayor, Craven Wallace appeared in one of the photos with Ms. Ashford, leading everyone to speculate to what other connections she had with the former mayor. According to sources, no one has any idea where the photos came from. A *Do Tail All* spokesperson claims the photos were delivered to them anonymously."

"Does someone have it in for the duplicitous Ms. Ashford? It would appear so. But the real question begs: Who hasn't this woman slept with?"

Landon felt light headed. *Oh my god! Is my photo going too pop-up next?*

He watched as photo after photo of Jess with different men appeared on the screen. He braced himself. If he was photographed with Jess, and his face was among those other men, what could that mean for him? As the news reporter stated, it was practically a done deal as far as Jess's career went. She wouldn't be able to show her face anywhere without being recognized. Her career was over. And Rafe, what about his career? He was supposed to be protecting Jess on that detail not screwing her. At the very least his wife would probably leave him. But the real concern made his heart beat faster when he thought of the implications for his own career.

Wanting to tear himself away from the screen, Landon found himself nailed to the spot, mesmerized. It was all so surreal. He felt like some masochist just standing there waiting for his certain punishment.

Chapter 30

Eric Valero stood in the doorway of his office watching a distraught Landon Payne. It was safe to say he was the only one to witness the emotions that played across the young officer's face. The others were too busy watching the fireworks on the television screens to pay him any attention. Finally, Landon gathered himself and turned to leave the building. Eric thought it was best. No one needed to know what was going on with him. He hoped the young man had 'suddenly become ill' and headed home; away from the prying eyes of his colleagues. With the burden of possible exposure weighing heavily upon him, it would be impossible for the others not to notice that something was wrong.

Eric turned and stepped back into his office, closing the door behind him. He would worry about Landon Payne later.

Picking up the Metro Gazette from his desk to a full color, front page exposé of Jess Ashford, he scanned the article. True to what he assumed all along, the media had gone nuts, demanding her head on a platter. Although the inappropriate body parts were blurred out, the faces of the participants in each photo were clearly visible *and* recognizable.

Eric rested his forehead on his open palms. He felt sorry for those whose lives would be impacted the most; the innocent families of the men involved. They would suffer greatly. The newspaper had only published some of the photos with promises of more to come. This only heightened the agony. The paper claimed there were just too many to post in one edition, which may be true. But he guessed the paper's underlying motive was to use the teaser as a ploy to sell more newspapers. And if human curiosity stayed true to form, it would undoubtedly work.

By the end of the week, every man Jess Ashford had ever been with will have had his face highlighted in some sensationalized manner. Although the Metro Gazette published the photos, with bodies covered, the original postings had already hit the internet without the dubious blur. The press was in a feeding frenzy. Eating up every detail and regurgitating it to the various scavengers around the world. By lunch, every news outlet imaginable would have copies of the photos plastered on their websites, with some highlighting the various uncovered parts and sexual positions for maximum shock value.

He also speculated there would be many marriages if not jobs lost that day, with more to follow as more photographs were revealed. One of the police departments own high ranking member had been dragged into the melee. It was a miracle that he had gotten a divorce the previous year or his marriage too would be among the casualties. Eric vaguely wondered if Jess Ashford had triggered that union's demise. Although Terrance Hanlon may have had an affair with Jess, his job would be safe, unlike Rafe Santiago's. His chosen security detail was in place to protect the district attorney. Sleeping with Jess jeopardized that security. Had someone been gunning for the DA, while they were rolling around in the sack, they both could have been killed. The police commission viewed this as a complete dereliction of duty and fired him immediately.

Eric looked up from the paper at a knock on his office door. He asked his visitor to enter. He hoped it wasn't more bad news.

Kobe stepped inside, closing the door behind him. He nodded towards the common room. "I see someone has been busy since I've been gone," he told Eric.

"Yeah, they have. The D. A.'s phone hasn't stopped ringing since this hit the news, with most of the callers wanting Jess fired without delay."

"Well, we were afraid this would happen and now it has. The woman doesn't deserve this. What goes on in her private life shouldn't matter." Kobe shook his head. He felt sorry for her.

"I totally agree, but what can we do?" Eric shrugged. "I know you didn't come here to discuss Jess Ashford's woes. What did you find on the west coast?"

"More than I cared to know," he muttered. Kobe took one of the chairs near Eric's desk to share his experiences in visiting the sex clubs, including why he was glad he hadn't taken KT along.

"You're right, I wouldn't have liked it one bit if KT had gone with you. That was a great call on your part. I knew that lifestyle was questionable, but geesh." Eric was just as appalled as Kobe had been over the sexual lives of some people.

"Well, I did come across a name that might help us in our search. James Harrison had a live in girlfriend before he moved here. And you're not going to believe who she is." Kobe was amused at Eric's piqued interest. He was shocked to learn the identity of James' lady friend and knew Eric would be too.

"I know her?" Eric asked.

"You're familiar with her, yes." Kobe couldn't contain his excitement, as Eric tried to guess who the mystery woman was.

"Does she live here in Metro City?" Kobe nodded. Eric concluded it couldn't be Jess, the world already knew all her secrets.

"Okay, you're going to have to go ahead and tell me because I don't have a clue."

"Dr. Lara Guyton," Kobe revealed.

Eric sat forward in his chair. "The neurosurgeon Lara Guyton? The one that went nuts and tried to stab Jon Payne in the midst of surgery Lara Guyton?"

Kobe nodded. "The one and only.

"Get the hell out of here!" He was shocked indeed.

"How the hell did they end up in Metro City? Did they come together?"

Kobe shook his head. "From what I could gather, they came here separately. Dr. Guyton told a friend she *had* to leave. The woman told me Lara couldn't endure anymore of James' sadistic sex games. She and the woman became friends after she moved in next door to her and James. I guess she needed to confide in someone." Kobe shrugged.

Kobe let that sink in before continuing. "James Harrison isn't just your garden variety, mild mannered sexual deviant; he likes to inflict a lot of pain to get his kicks. Lara told the friend, she thought she could handle it at first, but after a while, he became so out of control, she had to leave. So she skipped town and came here. And I'm assuming the skipping town part was intentional, in light of what I've learned about Harrison. I'm pretty sure he wouldn't have willingly allowed her to just leave, not without consequences."

"Is that why he landed here too? Following, or should I say searching for her?"

"Yes. Somehow he found out she was in the area and made the move. He hooked up with some of the clubs here and started quietly inquiring as to her precise whereabouts. But I'm assuming again, he didn't find her through the clubs, because no one recognized her photo and told him as much. She may have given up the old life and laid low. Especially if she thought James was looking for her."

"So, did he find her?"

"Of that I'm not sure. When I showed his photo around Metro Regional, no one seemed to recognize him. And I asked if anyone had called inquiring about her employment there, but no go there either. So if he did find her, I'm assuming it wasn't through the hospital."

Eric was quiet for a full minute; his mind was turning. If he did find her, shouldn't she be the one missing and not him? "Where is Dr. Guyton now? Is she still institutionalized?"

Kobe shook his head. "She's been out for weeks. According to the hospital administrator, she was released after satisfactory treatment and recovery; shortly resigning her position thereafter. One of the stipulations for her release was no contact with Jon Payne and she has been honoring that. In fact, and this is according to the hospital administrator, she packed up and left town."

"Oh, and I did speak to Dr. Payne. He said he saw her once after her release and hasn't seen her since. She came to apologize and that was it. He assumes she left town like she said she would."

Eric slowly shook his head. Something wasn't right. If James found Lara, why would he just up and disappear like that? He remembered Jess telling him; anything that could draw attention to their lifestyle was always deftly avoided. So if James Harrison wanted to retaliate against his former girlfriend, wouldn't he keep up appearances and go along as if nothing was happening? But the situation was just the opposite. He seemed to have vanished without a trace.

"Have you verified Dr. Guyton's whereabouts?

"I came here after leaving the hospital." Kobe shrugged. "As far as I know she left town."

Eric held up an index finger while he scooped up his desk phone to make a call. "Yes, this is Detective Valero at headquarters. Could you run an activity analysis on Dr. Lara Guyton's credit and debit cards for the last two months…oh and get me an address and get back to me ASAP? Thanks."

To Kobe, "While we wait, is there anything else that can make some sense as to what happened to him?"

"That's about all I have. And I know you've already thought of this, but wouldn't it be smart for Harrison to keep a high profile if he was somewhere offing his girlfriend? Besides, he doesn't grab me as the type to let things linger this long. I could see him taking her somewhere, killing her and burying her between court appearances." Kobe thought something else was going on here, but what?

Eric gently rocked in his chair. "Yeah that crossed my mind too." He stopped rocking to pick up the phone on the first ring. "Yes," he nodded as the caller relayed the information he requested. Cradling the phone between his ear and shoulder, he quickly grabbed a pen and pad; jotting down the message. "Thanks." Eric rose as he replaced the receiver.

"Lara Guyton is still in town. Her debit card was used as recently as yesterday to purchase some yarn from a craft store not far from her house. Let's go have a talk with her. Maybe she can help us find James."

He followed Kobe out the door. Maybe now they could get some answers.

Chapter 31

Jess Ashford sat cross-legged in the middle of her queen sized bed; silently taking in the circus that was currently being performed outside her home and on the national news outlet she was watching. She didn't have to wonder why news vans from all over had started pulling up to the curb, with reporters scrambling all over her lawn. She knew they had found out. And to bring the point further home, emails and voicemails had instantly flooded her phone's inboxes. The world had discovered her secret.

She knew it was coming and had prepared herself for the melee. She had already faxed the resignation she had prepared days ago to the mayor's office that morning. After the news hit the airwaves, there wasn't much of an explanation needed as to why she was resigning. Besides, she wanted to go out with some dignity, by counteracting her firing.

Her next step was to leave the city. But first she had to figure out a way to leave her home unmolested by the growing horde of vultures outside. The air was heavy with the smell of blood and the scavengers were waiting to devour her if they could. She was going to do everything in her power to make sure that didn't happen. But how?

Jess sighed and got up from the bed. She had been dressed for hours. Her suitcases were packed and all she needed now was an escape plan. She was contemplating one when like magic there was a slight tap on her bedroom window. She was about to go off, thinking it was a reporter when a friendly face appeared. It was Landon.

Surprised, she moved quickly to the floor to ceiling window; unlocking it before pushing it up to its full height.

"Landon, what are you doing here?" He was one of the last people she expected to see.

Removing the window screen, he climbed through the open window. "I thought you might need some help getting out of here."

He thought about not coming. After all, he was one of her lovers and probably everyone knew it by now. He should have been distancing himself from her, but he just couldn't leave her alone to fend off the press by herself.

"I parked my squad car over on the next street and since your backyard shares a fence with your neighbor's, we'll have to climb it to get to the car."

Jess glanced at her packed bags. She would have to leave them behind and send for them later. Grabbing her purse and one of the smaller totes, she tucked a floppy hat under her arm and followed Landon back through the window. She praised her decision to move into a neighborhood with high privacy fences. No one would be the wiser that she'd left via the backyard.

Racing across the expertly landscaped enclosure, Landon helped her over the back fence into the neighbor's equally cared for back garden. It was sheer luck no one was home to see them crossing the fence. They made their way through that yard, picking their way along another privacy fence to the street, where Landon looked in both directions to make sure they hadn't been seen. Satisfied they weren't being followed, they hurried down the block to the waiting patrol car. Once inside, Jess laid prone on the back seat. They had escaped her would be prison without being caught.

Landon looked over his shoulder and nodded at her, before shifting the car into drive and pulling from the curb. Now he just had to devise a plan to get her out of Metro City.

Chapter 32

James didn't know how many times he'd passed out during and after Lara's attack. He lost count after the first few blackouts. The muffled screams had initially stopped also. He just didn't have the energy left to lift his head, let alone to scream.

Now he had to endure the god awful stitching she was currently administering to his mangled chest. It wasn't crazy enough that she had sliced him up, and let the wounds lay open overnight, but now she was torturing him more, by closing them with florescent colored knitting yarn; alternately humming and singing with each agonizing stitch. But because of the initial attack, his body had become somewhat numb. At least he could be grateful for that. It was the constant pulling and tugging of the yarn being drawn through his flesh that was freaking him out now. It was as if he were a live corpse being sewn together after some bizarre autopsy.

Lara Guyton had managed to carve her name into every available space on James' bare chest. She had taken great care in placing the tip of the blade into his flesh, so not to allow too many of the cuttings to go too deep. Just enough to inflict maximum pain. There were a few times when she got carried away, and had to halt her handy work to stop the profuse bleeding. But once she stopped the annoying blood flow, she just picked up where she left off. The skilled surgeon was fully aware she could have used one of her scalpels, but that would have been much too pleasant for the likes of 'Dr. Jon Payne'.

Lara, finally placing her last stitch, tied it off, and rose from her kneeling position to admire her finished masterpiece. Pleased with her work, she gleefully clasped her hands together while twirling in a tight circle. As an afterthought, she stopped her turning to pinch a corner of the Duct tape covering 'Jon's' mouth, before ripping it and some of his skin away. She thought it would be a nice gesture to treat him to some cool water. Sewing up wounds was painstaking work, so he deserved something to quench his throat from all that screaming and moaning.

With some effort, James managed to lift his head to drink greedily from the steady stream being poured from a blue squeeze bottle; the kind that had a built-in filter on top to purify the liquid before drinking it. At this point, he didn't care if the water came from the sewer. His throat was raw and it hurt like hell, but it was paramount that he satisfied his thirst. It had been days since Lara had given him any food or water; leaving his body frail and dehydrated. After drinking his fill, he closed his eyes and let his head drop forward again; grateful for any act of kindness she gave.

Feeling a little better, but with his head still hung low, James worked his lips to speak. "Have you had enough now Lara? Haven't you punished me enough?" he asked. His voice was weak and barely audible from the hoarseness; a mere imitation of its former robust timbre. Lara had cut all the fight out of him. He just wanted her to be done and let him go. He didn't care if he died afterwards; he just wanted to be far away from her crazed house of horrors. He just wanted some peace.

Lara considered 'Jon' for a moment. He sounded so tired and so weary. Maybe she had done enough. One thing was for certain, Jon Payne would never forget her. She made certain of that. While she was considering releasing him, the doorbell rang.

James wept with relief. Someone had come to save him.

Eric rang Lara's doorbell while Kobe moved around the side of the house, peering into every uncovered window. When he got to the patio doors around back, he was horrified at what he saw. Panicking, he picked up the nearest heavy object, sending it crashing through the sliding glass doors.

Hearing the crash, Eric drew his gun before kicking open the front door; checking every nook and open doorway, as he made his way through the house. He called out to Kobe.

"In here!"

Still cautious, he picked his way through the house towards the direction of Kobe's voice, letting his Glock 22 lead the way. When he stepped into the dining room, the scene was one that would haunt him for years to come. There sat James Harrison, strapped to a chair with his chest covered in dozens of angry, red cuts held together by bright orange yarn, and he was weeping. Eric managed to tear his gaze from an openly grateful James, to glance in the direction of an equally horrified Kobe. Kobe was staring down at Lara Guyton, who had seated herself on the carpeted floor with her legs folded under her. She was gently humming while she rocked back and forth.

Holstering his gun, Eric couldn't shake Kobe's puzzled gaze that was silently asking, 'What the hell happened here?'

He had no words; he could only shake his head from side to side, for what seemed like minutes, in disbelief. Neither of them had ever seen anything like it. It took him a moment to realize he needed to call into the station and for an ambulance to get James some help. He didn't know where to begin explaining this scene.

While Eric made the necessary calls, Kobe got Lara to her feet and cuffed her before seating her in one of the chairs opposite James. He didn't think she would cause any more harm, but it was reassuring for him that she was restrained just the same.

Lara looked over at James and grinned. "I did you up good didn't I Jon? Didn't I?" she grinned some more before she started repeating, "No pain, no gain for Jon Payne." She repeated this mantra, while she continued her rocking.

Chapter 33

"Well, Jocelyn, just when we thought we had stuffed ourselves with all the scandal we could handle, even more has been added to our plate." This was a field reporter conversing with his news station's anchor, concerning the kidnapping and mutilation of James Harrison.

"That's right Ted. What is this city coming to?" Jocelyn replied. "Can you tell us where you are and a little bit about what happened there?"

Ted was more than obliged to inform her and their viewing audience on the latest. "Well, Jocelyn, I'm standing in front of Dr. Lara Guyton's home that has now been dubbed 'Lara's House of Horrors', because of the unspeakable things she did to…"

Jon Payne muted the television and turned to Detective Eric Valero. His hands were shakings. He had the unfortunate task of witnessing Lara's madness up close a second time. Ironically, he was the only available physician on duty when the paramedics wheeled James Harrison into the emergency department, near hysterics. And now the detective was telling him, *he* was the intended target of Dr. Guyton's little slicing party.

"So when she saw Harrison outside her home, she thought it was me?"

Eric nodded. He told Jon about James and Lara's relationship prior to them coming to Metro City and how James happened to be there spying on her when she surprised him, by drugging him and dragging him into the house. He explained how Lara had kept him drugged until she carved up his chest as punishment for Jon's abandonment of her.

"All of this occurred because she'd slipped back into her psychosis," Eric continued. "From what her psychiatrist could gather, she stopped taking her medication right before being released; maybe a week or so. It was the only rationalization that explained her rapid backslide. And although she kept her scheduled appointments thereafter, somehow she managed to appear quite sane."

"But didn't they think something was wrong when she stopped showing up for her appointments," Jon asked. He couldn't understand how this much madness had gone undetected for so long.

"As you may remember, Dr. Guyton was supposed to have left town. So when she discontinued her appointments, her doctor just assumed she'd left and picked up her therapy with the physician he recommended in her new city. Unfortunately, no one bothered to follow up to see if she had actually checked in with the new doctor; leaving her free and clear to do whatever she pleased."

Jon swiped a shaky hand down his face. He saw what Lara did to James Harrison and he was having a difficult time coming to grips with the fact that it could have been him she cut up. And had Lara recognized that James wasn't her intended target, it would have been him. There was no doubt in his mind she would have found a way to have him on the receiving end of that butcher's knife. Not to mention being stitched back together with that hideous orange yarn. It took him and his team awhile to remove it all and stitch him up properly. And he knows for certain that James Harrison was more than grateful he was under anesthesia this time, feeling no pain or discomfort at all.

Unfortunately, because of the gashes being left unattended for so long, he would have one hell of a reminder with all the scars Lara purposefully left behind—

physically and mentally. James Harrison would never be the same again.

Landon watched from his car as the private jet lifted off into the darkening sky. Jess Ashford had procured a private international flight that took her to parts unknown. He hadn't asked where she was headed and she hadn't volunteered the information. He just hoped wherever she landed she would find peace.

After they made it out of her neighborhood without being seen or followed, Landon took her to his place where he swapped out the patrol car for his own personal vehicle. He had driven directly into the two car garage, pressing the release button for the door to lower as soon as the car cleared it. Jess didn't emerge from her hiding spot until the garage door was securely closed. On the ride over to his place, she had questioned him again why he was helping her. Although he may not have agreed with her lifestyle, he didn't think it was right what someone was doing to her.

While he changed into civilian clothes, he heard Jess on the phone making flight reservations in a neighboring city. They both knew the press would probably be camped out at Metro City's airport. Some were there waiting just in case they missed her at her home.

He had already informed the station he would be out for a family emergency for a couple of days. With all the chaos and attention surrounding the outing of so many of Jess's sex partners, the desk sergeant could have cared less. He could have told him he was going into labor and he wouldn't have blinked an eye. The sergeant was too engrossed in the drama that was unfolding on the news to be bothered with his personal leave time. It seemed the entire city had halted its routine to watch the train wreck. Even the criminals had ceased their activities for the moment.

Landon breathed a sigh of relief. So far, neither his or Jon's name *or* face, for that matter, had been connected to Jess. He knew his reprieve was probably short lived, considering the news outlets were promising to publish more as the days went by. But according to the news cast this morning, *all* of the photos had been posted by *Do Tail All*, which could very well mean he, as well as Jon, was among them. But if they were, why hadn't his phone rang? It hadn't rung not even once since this madness began. It should have been blowing up by now.

Getting back into his car, he made a mental note to check the website himself when he got home, and hoped against all hope that he had been spared the circus.

Chapter 34

Nurse Shelby Kirkland froze when she was asked to hand Dr. Payne the defibrillator pads. They were losing their patient. When it was clear that Shelby was unable to fulfill his request, he nodded at another nurse who gently nudged Shelby aside to hand the paddles to him. Jon had to apply them to the man's chest twice before his heartbeat returned.

Realizing she had skipped out mentally, Shelby turned on her heels and hurried from the room. She didn't stop until she reached the emergency stairwell where she made her way three floors down, before she sat on the steps to cry. When the patient went into cardiac arrest, all she could think about was her brother and how she was so angry with him. She never got a chance to tell him she still loved him even though he left her. Shelby was so distraught with grief that she didn't hear Jon coming down the stairs. She wasn't aware of him until he sat down beside her and gathered her into his arms.

After the patient was stabilized, he went to the nurses' station to find her. He caught the attention of a nurse on the phone, who pointed towards the stairwell, indicating that she was there. It was a popular spot for the staff when they needed some alone time.

He held Shelby while she released a lifetime of pent up anger and grief. Jon knew the time would come when the death of her brother would hit her. And as promised, he was there for her and would be for as long as she needed him.

Gathering her emotions, Shelby relaxed completely in Jon's embrace. It had been a long time since anyone had held her. As far as she remembered, the last person who held her was her grandmother.

"You want to talk about it?" Jon asked, after he felt her relax.

Without moving from his embrace, she nodded. "Before my brother died, I was so angry with him. Now I will never get a chance to make things right between us." Shelby sighed. If she hadn't let her pride get in the way, she and Alonso could have made amends and possibly been there for each other.

"Why were you angry?" Jon placed his chin atop her head. Neither one wanting to release the other.

"Alonso and I were left to live with our grandmother growing up. I was very young and have no memory of our parents, so aside from my grandmother, he was the only connection I had to them and he just up and left one day and never came back. I needed my brother and he just left. I came home from school and all of his things were gone. I asked Nana what happen, but she only shrugged. From the way the place was torn up, I could guess she and Alonso had argued about our parents again."

Jon looked at her then. "I don't understand."

"Neither did I. And I still don't. Our parents had always been a sore subject with us. Alonso refused to discuss them and Nana only mentioned our father in hushed tones when Alonso wasn't around. It made him angry whenever she talked about her only son. I don't know anything about my mother not even her name."

"So your father just left you there?" Jon was astonished.

Shelby nodded. "From what I could gather from my grandmother, my father just showed up one day with the two of us in tow and left us there without explanation. We never saw him again. Because I was so young, I can't even remember what he looks like. And any photos my grandmother had were destroyed by Alonso. He hated anything that had to do with our father."

Jon couldn't believe what he was hearing. What kind of parents just abandoned their kids like that? As he listened to the pain that colored Shelby's voice he vowed to help her find her folks. Her estranged brother was the only family connection she had and now he was gone. Shelby needed her family and if it were at all possible, he would help her find them.

Chapter 35

Eric carefully and thoroughly shredded the photos he kept safely hidden in a locked box in his desk drawer. He'd held onto them long enough. Even though he knew there were probably copies of them out there somewhere, those men in the photos would never know they were ever in his possession. They were good men, whom he knew well. They didn't deserve to have their lives torn apart by some evil bastard with an axe to grind against Jess Ashford. He just hated he couldn't include the one with James Harrison. The man had already been through enough, but unfortunately for him, he would have to endure more. If he hadn't included his photo, KT and Kobe would have known right off the bat he was the one who leaked them. But then again, after all James had been through, he may be the one person the scandal wouldn't taint. The man was grateful just to be alive.

Eric knew it was risky sending the batch of photos to the scandal website, but he had to do it if he was to try to protect the men. It was just a matter of time before Jess's enemy pulled his or her trump card and unleashed *all* of the photos on the world. This way, he had some control over who would be outed and who wouldn't. He just hoped the person responsible for the whole mess didn't have a vendetta against the two men in the destroyed photos.

The three photos destroyed, were images of Landon and his brother Jon depicting their time with Jess. The third showed the two brothers in Jess's bedroom together. Although he didn't think the photo implied a threesome, Eric knew that would be the Medias' first conclusion. From his point of view, it looked like a confrontation, which would be equally damaging. He could just see the headlines: 'Payne Brothers Fight over Trashy DA'.

He didn't know Jon to the extent that he knew his brother, but he would protect him just the same. From all accounts, Dr. Jon Payne was a fine surgeon and a good man. And as for Landon, if those photos were to surface, he would never become detective; a promotion Eric thought he richly deserved. So for now, the brothers Payne were safe. And if other photos with the three ever resurfaced…well he would just have to deal with it then.

When the task was finished, Eric sighed. No one could ever know he was the one who leaked the batch. He would take that secret to the grave. He was glad he had removed them from the pile before his fiancé or Kobe had a look at them. Although it was impossible to remember

every face, Jon and Landon's would have certainly stood
out.

Grateful that Jess Ashford's downfall was behind
them, at least for now, Eric turned to his latest
investigation. Who killed Alonso Kane?

Jess Ashford's enemy watched the media circus on
one of the local news channels with a half-smile. It was the
third day of Jess's scandal. His eyes danced while photo
after photo appeared on the large screen. He wasn't upset
with the detective for leaking the photographs. On the
contrary, he thought it was a brilliant move and applauded
him for it. After all, the man had integrity and protected his
friends. Eric Valero was loyal. He liked that.

It hadn't mattered to him that some of the photos
were held back. The men who were exposed were just a
means to an end. It was Jess Ashford he wanted to hurt;
everyone else was regretfully collateral damage. He had
bested that bitch and that was all that mattered.

And just to show the detective there were no hard
feelings he retrieved the original photos of the men from
his safe and shredded them also; sending the clippings to
Eric with a note reassuring him that his friends were safe

from him. The Payne brothers could continue their lives unmolested.

Jess's enemy leaned back into his comfortable chair and lit a Cuban cigar. He had been saving the treat for just the right moment and it had finally come. That uppity bitch had finally received her comeuppance with the help of his truly and he couldn't have been more pleased. He knew having friends in low places would pay off someday. And his friendship with the disgraced priest had certainly paid off in a mighty way.

After Father Mason Coburn was exposed in the human trafficking sting, that also netted the top officials of Metro City, he had secretly turned to him for counsel, neither knowing their connection would be the key to take down the lady prosecutor. Jess may not have had a relationship with the priest, but Coburn knew plenty who had. Over the years, Mason Coburn had managed to film or collect photos of personal sexual encounters of his *and* those of his associates. He liked to keep mementoes just in case someone in his sadistic inner circle had the mind to step out of line. He used his arsenal as a gentle reminder as to who was truly in control.

After the charges were dropped, Coburn gifted him the compilation, as appreciation for the legal advice that enabled him to avoid prosecution *and* jail time. When Mason discovered his hatred for Jess, he forwarded stills from every video he had of her and her playmates. And after receiving the gold mine, more photos were added to the collection by way of a recently acquired collaborator who kept close tabs on the woman's sexual escapades shortly after she landed in Metro City. The cohort was enticed with the promise of a healthy bonus, if he could plant cameras in her home and office. The money he paid the man was well spent.

Now, because of his efforts, the world knew what a whore Jess Ashford was. And by the time the media finished tearing her apart she wouldn't be able to snag a job as city dog catcher.

Liked *Payne before Pleasure*? Read the next book in the Metro City series, *A Queen's Choice*, to continue the mystery and drama.

Find Other Books by Katrina

@

Amazon.com

BarnesandNoble.com

Also Read book by Katrina's Alter-Ego Author

Olivia M. Dutton:

Mama Said Keep Your Dress Tail Down

What Mama Should Have Said

Where was God?

Olivia's Books on

Amazon

www.ingramcontent.com/pod-product-compliance
Lightning Source LLC
Chambersburg PA
CBHW051511170626
46811CB00002B/751